THE DUEL
&
COLONEL CHABERT

When Lieutenant D'Hubert is sent to arrest Lieutenant Feraud for wounding a civilian in a duel, Feraud truculently insists on fighting the other officer — sparking a deadly feud between the two Hussars which will erupt in recurrent duels across many miles and many years . . . The japes of the law-clerks in the office of M. Derville are interrupted by the arrival of an old man in a tattered box-coat, seeking the attorney. He claims he is Chabert — the brave cavalry Colonel, beloved by Napoleon, who was presumed slain at Eylau. And he wants M. Derville to win back the money and honour stolen away from him . . .

Books by Joseph Conrad
Published by Ulverscroft:

LORD JIM
HEART OF DARKNESS
THE END OF THE TETHER
THE SECRET AGENT

JOSEPH CONRAD &
HONORÉ DE BALZAC

◆

THE DUEL
&
COLONEL CHABERT

Complete and Unabridged

ULVERSCROFT
Leicester

The Duel — Joseph Conrad
First published in Great Britain in 1908

Colonel Chabert — Honoré de Balzac
First published in France in 1832,
under the title *La Transaction*
This translation, by Ellen Marriage and Clara Bell,
first published in Great Britain in 1901

This Large Print Edition
published 2017

*A catalogue record for this book is available
from the British Library.*

ISBN 978–1–4448–3477–2

Published by
F. A. Thorpe (Publishing)
Anstey, Leicestershire

Set by Words & Graphics Ltd.
Anstey, Leicestershire
Printed and bound in Great Britain by
T. J. International Ltd., Padstow, Cornwall

This book is printed on acid-free paper

Contents

Contents

THE DUEL

A Military Tale

Les petites marionnettes
Font, font, font,
Trois petits tours
Et puis s'en vont.

— NURSERY RHYME

TO MISS M.H.M. CAPES

1

Napoleon I., whose career had the quality of a duel against the whole of Europe, disliked duelling between the officers of his army. The great military emperor was not a swashbuckler, and had little respect for tradition.

Nevertheless, a story of duelling, which became a legend in the army, runs through the epic of imperial wars. To the surprise and admiration of their fellows, two officers, like insane artists trying to gild refined gold or paint the lily, pursued a private contest through the years of universal carnage. They were officers of cavalry, and their connection with the high-spirited but fanciful animal which carries men into battle seems particularly appropriate. It would be difficult to imagine for heroes of this legend two officers of infantry of the line, for example, whose fantasy is tamed by much walking exercise, and whose valour necessarily must be of a more plodding kind. As to gunners or engineers, whose heads are kept cool on a diet of mathematics, it is simply unthinkable.

The names of the two officers were Feraud and D'Hubert, and they were both lieutenants in a regiment of hussars, but not in the same regiment.

Feraud was doing regimental work, but Lieut. D'Hubert had the good fortune to be attached to the person of the general commanding the division, as officier d'ordonnance. It was in Strasbourg, and in this agreeable and important garrison they were enjoying greatly a short interval of peace. They were enjoying it, though both intensely warlike, because it was a sword-sharpening, firelock-cleaning peace, dear to a military heart and undamaging to military prestige, inasmuch that no one believed in its sincerity or duration.

Under those historical circumstances, so favourable to the proper appreciation of military leisure, Lieut. D'Hubert, one fine afternoon, made his way along a quiet street of a cheerful suburb towards Lieut. Feraud's quarters, which were in a private house with a garden at the back, belonging to an old maiden lady.

His knock at the door was answered instantly by a young maid in Alsatian costume. Her fresh complexion and her long eyelashes, lowered demurely at the sight of the tall officer, caused Lieut. D'Hubert, who was accessible to esthetic impressions, to relax the cold, severe gravity of his face. At the same time he observed that the girl had over her arm a pair of hussar's breeches, blue with a red stripe.

'Lieut. Feraud in?' he inquired, benevolently.

'Oh, no, sir! He went out at six this morning.'

The pretty maid tried to close the door. Lieut. D'Hubert, opposing this move with gentle firmness, stepped into the ante-room, jingling his spurs.

'Come, my dear! You don't mean to say he has not been home since six o'clock this morning?'

Saying these words, Lieut. D'Hubert opened without ceremony the door of a room so comfortably and neatly ordered that only from internal evidence in the shape of boots, uniforms, and military accoutrements did he acquire the conviction that it was Lieut. Feraud's room. And he saw also that Lieut. Feraud was not at home. The truthful maid had followed him, and raised her candid eyes to his face.

'H'm!' said Lieut. D'Hubert, greatly disappointed, for he had already visited all the haunts where a lieutenant of hussars could be found of a fine afternoon. 'So he's out? And do you happen to know, my dear, why he went out at six this morning?'

'No,' she answered, readily. 'He came home late last night, and snored. I heard him when I got up at five. Then he dressed himself in his oldest uniform and went out. Service, I suppose.'

'Service? Not a bit of it!' cried Lieut. D'Hubert. 'Learn, my angel, that he went out thus early to fight a duel with a civilian.'

She heard this news without a quiver of her dark eyelashes. It was very obvious that the actions of Lieut. Feraud were generally above criticism. She only looked up for a moment in mute surprise, and Lieut. D'Hubert concluded from this absence of emotion that she must have seen Lieut. Feraud since the morning. He looked around the room.

'Come!' he insisted, with confidential familiarity. 'He's perhaps somewhere in the house now?'

She shook her head.

'So much the worse for him!' continued Lieut. D'Hubert, in a tone of anxious conviction. 'But he has been home this morning.'

This time the pretty maid nodded slightly.

'He has!' cried Lieut. D'Hubert. 'And went out again? What for? Couldn't he keep quietly indoors! What a lunatic! My dear girl — '

Lieut. D'Hubert's natural kindness of disposition and strong sense of comradeship helped his powers of observation. He changed his tone to a most insinuating softness, and, gazing at the hussar's breeches hanging over

8

the arm of the girl, he appealed to the interest she took in Lieut. Feraud's comfort and happiness. He was pressing and persuasive. He used his eyes, which were kind and fine, with excellent effect. His anxiety to get hold at once of Lieut. Feraud, for Lieut. Feraud's own good, seemed so genuine that at last it overcame the girl's unwillingness to speak. Unluckily she had not much to tell. Lieut. Feraud had returned home shortly before ten, had walked straight into his room, and had thrown himself on his bed to resume his slumbers. She had heard him snore rather louder than before far into the afternoon. Then he got up, put on his best uniform, and went out. That was all she knew.

She raised her eyes, and Lieut. D'Hubert stared into them incredulously.

'It's incredible. Gone parading the town in his best uniform! My dear child, don't you know he ran that civilian through this morning? Clean through, as you spit a hare.'

The pretty maid heard the gruesome intelligence without any signs of distress. But she pressed her lips together thoughtfully.

'He isn't parading the town,' she remarked in a low tone. 'Far from it.'

'The civilian's family is making an awful row,' continued Lieut. D'Hubert, pursuing his train of thought. 'And the general is very angry. It's one of the best families in the town. Feraud ought to have kept close at least — '

'What will the general do to him?' inquired the girl, anxiously.

'He won't have his head cut off, to be sure,' grumbled Lieut. D'Hubert. 'His conduct is positively indecent. He's making no end of trouble for himself by this sort of bravado.'

'But he isn't parading the town,' the maid insisted in a shy murmur.

'Why, yes! Now I think of it, I haven't seen him anywhere about. What on earth has he done with himself?'

'He's gone to pay a call,' suggested the maid, after a moment of silence.

Lieut. D'Hubert started.

'A call! Do you mean a call on a lady? The cheek of the man! And how do you know this, my dear?'

Without concealing her woman's scorn for the denseness of the masculine mind, the pretty maid reminded him that Lieut. Feraud had arrayed himself in his best uniform before going out. He had also put on his newest dolman, she added, in a tone as if this conversation were getting on her nerves, and turned away brusquely.

Lieut. D'Hubert, without questioning the accuracy of the deduction, did not see that it advanced him much on his official quest. For his quest after Lieut. Feraud had an official character. He did not know any of the women this fellow, who had run a man through in the morning, was likely to visit in the afternoon. The two young men knew each other but slightly. He bit his gloved finger in perplexity.

'Call!' he exclaimed. 'Call on the devil!'

The girl, with her back to him, and folding the hussars breeches on a chair, protested with a vexed little laugh:

'Oh, dear, no! On Madame de Lionne.'

Lieut. D'Hubert whistled softly. Madame de Lionne was the wife of a high official who had a well-known salon and some pretensions to sensibility and elegance. The husband was a civilian, and old; but the society of the salon was young and military. Lieut. D'Hubert had whistled, not because the idea of pursuing Lieut. Feraud into that very salon was disagreeable to him, but because, having arrived in Strasbourg only lately, he had not had the time as yet to get an introduction to Madame de Lionne. And what was that swashbuckler Feraud doing there, he wondered. He did not seem the sort of man who —

'Are you certain of what you say?' asked Lieut. D'Hubert.

The girl was perfectly certain. Without

11

turning round to look at him, she explained that the coachman of their next door neighbours knew the maitre-d'hotel of Madame de Lionne. In this way she had her information. And she was perfectly certain. In giving this assurance she sighed. Lieut. Feraud called there nearly every afternoon, she added.

'Ah, bah!' exclaimed D'Hubert, ironically. His opinion of Madame de Lionne went down several degrees. Lieut. Feraud did not seem to him specially worthy of attention on the part of a woman with a reputation for sensibility and elegance. But there was no saying. At bottom they were all alike — very practical rather than idealistic. Lieut. D'Hubert, however, did not allow his mind to dwell on these considerations.

'By thunder!' he reflected aloud. 'The general goes there sometimes. If he happens to find the fellow making eyes at the lady there will be the devil to pay! Our general is not a very accommodating person, I can tell you.'

'Go quickly, then! Don't stand here now I've told you where he is!' cried the girl, colouring to the eyes.

'Thanks, my dear! I don't know what I would have done without you.'

After manifesting his gratitude in an aggressive way, which at first was repulsed violently, and then submitted to with a sudden and still more repellent indifference, Lieut. D'Hubert took his departure.

He clanked and jingled along the streets with a martial swagger. To run a comrade to earth in a drawing-room where he was not known did not trouble him in the least. A uniform is a passport. His position as officier d'ordonnance of the general added to his assurance. Moreover, now that he knew where to find Lieut. Feraud, he had no option. It was a service matter.

Madame de Lionne's house had an excellent appearance. A man in livery, opening the door of a large drawing-room with a waxed floor, shouted his name and stood aside to let him pass. It was a reception day. The ladies wore big hats surcharged with a profusion of feathers; their bodies sheathed in clinging white gowns, from the armpits to the tips of the low satin shoes, looked sylph-like and cool in a great display of bare necks and arms. The men who talked with them, on the contrary, were arrayed heavily in multi-coloured garments with collars up to their ears and thick sashes round their waists. Lieut. D'Hubert made his unabashed way across the room and, bowing low before a sylph-like form reclining on a couch, offered his apologies for this intrusion, which nothing could excuse but the extreme urgency of the service order he had to communicate to his comrade Feraud. He proposed to himself to return presently in a more regular manner and beg forgiveness for interrupting the interesting conversation . . .

A bare arm was extended towards him with gracious nonchalance even before he had finished speaking. He pressed the hand respectfully to his lips, and made the mental remark that it was bony. Madame de Lionne was a blonde, with too fine a skin and a long face.

'C'est ca!' she said, with an ethereal smile, disclosing a set of large teeth. 'Come this evening to plead for your forgiveness.'

'I will not fail, madame.'

Meantime, Lieut. Feraud, splendid in his new dolman and the extremely polished boots of his calling, sat on a chair within a foot of the couch, one hand resting on his thigh, the other twirling his moustache to a point. At a significant glance from D'Hubert he rose without alacrity, and followed him into the recess of a window.

'What is it you want with me?' he asked, with astonishing indifference. Lieut. D'Hubert could not imagine that in the innocence of his heart and simplicity of his conscience Lieut. Feraud took a view of his duel in which neither remorse nor yet a rational apprehension of consequences had any place. Though he had no clear recollection how the quarrel had originated (it was begun in an establishment where beer and wine are drunk late at night), he had not the slightest doubt of being himself the outraged party. He had had two experienced friends for his seconds. Everything had been done according to the rules governing that sort of adventures. And a duel is obviously fought for the purpose of someone being at least hurt, if not killed outright. The civilian got hurt. That also was in order. Lieut. Feraud was perfectly tranquil; but Lieut. D'Hubert took it for affectation, and spoke with a certain vivacity.

'I am directed by the general to give you the order to go at once to your quarters, and remain there under close arrest.'

It was now the turn of Lieut. Feraud to be astonished. 'What the devil are you telling me there?' he murmured, faintly, and fell into such profound wonder that he could only follow mechanically the motions of Lieut. D'Hubert. The two officers, one tall, with an interesting face and a moustache the colour of ripe corn, the other, short and sturdy, with a hooked nose and a thick crop of black curly hair, approached the mistress of the house to take their leave. Madame de Lionne, a woman of eclectic taste, smiled upon these armed young men with impartial sensibility and an equal share of interest. Madame de Lionne took her delight in the infinite variety of the human species. All the other eyes in the drawing-room followed the departing officers; and when they had gone out one or two men, who had already heard of the duel, imparted the information to the sylph-like ladies, who received it with faint shrieks of humane concern.

Meantime, the two hussars walked side by side, Lieut. Feraud trying to master the hidden reason of things which in this instance eluded the grasp of his intellect, Lieut. D'Hubert feeling annoyed at the part he had to play, because the general's instructions were that he should see personally that Lieut. Feraud carried out his orders to the letter, and at once.

'The chief seems to know this animal,' he thought, eyeing his companion, whose round face, the round eyes, and even the twisted-up jet black little moustache seemed animated by a mental exasperation against the incomprehensible. And aloud he observed rather reproachfully, 'The general is in a devilish fury with you!'

Lieut. Feraud stopped short on the edge of the pavement, and cried in accents of unmistakable sincerity, 'What on earth for?' The innocence of the fiery Gascon soul was depicted in the manner in which he seized his head in both hands as if to prevent it bursting with perplexity.

'For the duel,' said Lieut. D'Hubert, curtly. He was annoyed greatly by this sort of perverse fooling.

'The duel! The . . . '

Lieut. Feraud passed from one paroxysm of astonishment into another. He dropped his hands and walked on slowly, trying to reconcile this information with the state of his own feelings. It was impossible. He burst out indignantly, 'Was I to let that sauerkraut-eating civilian wipe his boots on the uniform of the 7th Hussars?'

Lieut. D'Hubert could not remain altogether unmoved by that simple sentiment. This little fellow was a lunatic, he thought to himself, but there was something in what he said.

'Of course, I don't know how far you were justified,' he began, soothingly. 'And the general himself may not be exactly informed. Those people have been deafening him with their lamentations.'

'Ah! the general is not exactly informed,' mumbled Lieut. Feraud, walking faster and faster as his choler at the injustice of his fate began to rise. 'He is not exactly . . . And he orders me under close arrest, with God knows what afterwards!'

'Don't excite yourself like this,' remonstrated the other. 'Your adversary's people are very influential, you know, and it looks bad enough on the face of it. The general had to take notice of their complaint at once. I don't think he means to be over-severe with you. It's the best thing for you to be kept out of sight for a while.'

'I am very much obliged to the general,' muttered Lieut. Feraud through his teeth. 'And perhaps you would say I ought to be grateful to you, too, for the trouble you have taken to hunt me up in the drawing-room of a lady who — '

'Frankly,' interrupted Lieut. D'Hubert, with an innocent laugh, 'I think you ought to be. I had no end of trouble to find out where you were. It wasn't exactly the place for you to disport yourself in under the circumstances. If the general had caught you there making eyes at the goddess of the temple . . . oh, my word! . . . He hates to be bothered with complaints against his officers, you know. And it looked uncommonly like sheer bravado.'

The two officers had arrived now at the street door of Lieut. Feraud's lodgings. The latter turned towards his companion. 'Lieut. D'Hubert,' he said, 'I have something to say to you, which can't be said very well in the street. You can't refuse to come up.'

The pretty maid had opened the door. Lieut. Feraud brushed past her brusquely, and she raised her scared and questioning eyes to Lieut. D'Hubert, who could do nothing but shrug his shoulders slightly as he followed with marked reluctance.

In his room Lieut. Feraud unhooked the clasp, flung his new dolman on the bed, and, folding his arms across his chest, turned to the other hussar.

'Do you imagine I am a man to submit tamely to injustice?' he inquired, in a boisterous voice.

'Oh, do be reasonable!' remonstrated Lieut. D'Hubert.

'I am reasonable! I am perfectly reasonable!' retorted the other with ominous restraint. 'I can't call the general to account for his behaviour, but you are going to answer me for yours.'

'I can't listen to this nonsense,' murmured Lieut. D'Hubert, making a slightly contemptuous grimace.

'You call this nonsense? It seems to me a perfectly plain statement. Unless you don't understand French.'

'What on earth do you mean?'

'I mean,' screamed suddenly Lieut. Feraud, 'to cut off your ears to teach you to disturb me with the general's orders when I am talking to a lady!'

A profound silence followed this mad declaration; and through the open window Lieut. D'Hubert heard the little birds singing sanely in the garden. He said, preserving his calm, 'Why! If you take that tone, of course I shall hold myself at your disposition whenever you are at liberty to attend to this affair; but I don't think you will cut my ears off.'

'I am going to attend to it at once,' declared Lieut. Feraud, with extreme truculence. 'If you are thinking of displaying your airs and graces to-night in Madame de Lionne's salon you are very much mistaken.'

'Really!' said Lieut. D'Hubert, who was beginning to feel irritated, 'you are an impracticable sort of fellow. The general's orders to me were to put you under arrest, not to carve you into small pieces. Good-morning!' And turning his back on the little Gascon, who, always sober in his potations, was as though born intoxicated with the sunshine of his vine-ripening country, the Northman, who could drink hard on occasion, but was born sober under the watery skies of Picardy, made for the door.

Hearing, however, the unmistakable sound behind his back of a sword drawn from the scabbard, he had no option but to stop.

'Devil take this mad Southerner!' he thought, spinning round and surveying with composure the warlike posture of Lieut. Feraud, with a bare sword in his hand.

'At once! — at once!' stuttered Feraud, beside himself.

'You had my answer,' said the other, keeping his temper very well.

At first he had been only vexed, and somewhat amused; but now his face got clouded. He was asking himself seriously how he could manage to get away. It was impossible to run from a man with a sword, and as to fighting him, it seemed completely out of the question. He waited awhile, then said exactly what was in his heart.

'Drop this! I won't fight with you. I won't be made ridiculous.'

'Ah, you won't?' hissed the Gascon. 'I suppose you prefer to be made infamous. Do you hear what I say? . . . Infamous! Infamous! Infamous!' he shrieked, rising and falling on his toes and getting very red in the face.

Lieut. D'Hubert, on the contrary, became very pale at the sound of the unsavoury word for a moment, then flushed pink to the roots of his fair hair. 'But you can't go out to fight;

you are under arrest, you lunatic!' he objected, with angry scorn.

'There's the garden: it's big enough to layout your long carcass in,' spluttered the other with such ardour that somehow the anger of the cooler man subsided.

'This is perfectly absurd,' he said, glad enough to think he had found a way out of it for the moment. 'We shall never get any of our comrades to serve as seconds. It's preposterous.'

'Seconds! Damn the seconds! We don't want any seconds. Don't you worry about any seconds. I shall send word to your friends to come and bury you when I am done. And if you want any witnesses, I'll send word to the old girl to put her head out of a window at the back. Stay! There's the gardener. He'll do. He's as deaf as a post, but he has two eyes in his head. Come along! I will teach you, my staff officer, that the carrying about of a general's orders is not always child's play.'

While thus discoursing he had unbuckled his empty scabbard. He sent it flying under the bed, and, lowering the point of the sword, brushed past the perplexed Lieut. D'Hubert, exclaiming, 'Follow me!' Directly he had flung open the door a faint shriek was heard and the pretty maid, who had been listening at the keyhole, staggered away, putting the backs of her hands over her eyes. Feraud did not seem to see her, but she ran after him and seized his left arm. He shook her off, and then she rushed towards Lieut. D'Hubert and clawed at the sleeve of his uniform.

'Wretched man!' she sobbed. 'Is this what you wanted to find him for?'

'Let me go,' entreated Lieut. D'Hubert, trying to disengage himself gently. 'It's like being in a madhouse,' he protested, with exasperation. 'Do let me go! I won't do him any harm.'

A fiendish laugh from Lieut. Feraud commented that assurance. 'Come along!' he shouted, with a stamp of his foot.

And Lieut. D'Hubert did follow. He could do nothing else. Yet in vindication of his sanity it must be recorded that as he passed through the ante-room the notion of opening the street door and bolting out presented itself to this brave youth, only of course to be instantly dismissed, for he felt sure that the other would pursue him without shame or compunction. And the prospect of an officer of hussars being chased along the street by another officer of hussars with a naked sword could not be for a moment entertained. Therefore he followed into the garden. Behind them the girl tottered out, too. With ashy lips and wild, scared eyes, she surrendered herself to a dreadful curiosity. She had also the notion of rushing if need be between Lieut. Feraud and death.

The deaf gardener, utterly unconscious of approaching footsteps, went on watering his flowers till Lieut. Feraud thumped him on the back. Beholding suddenly an enraged man flourishing a big sabre, the old chap trembling in all his limbs dropped the watering-pot. At once Lieut. Feraud kicked it away with great animosity, and, seizing the gardener by the throat, backed him against a tree. He held him there, shouting in his ear, 'Stay here, and look on! You understand? You've got to look on! Don't dare budge from the spot!'

Lieut. D'Hubert came slowly down the walk, unclasping his dolman with unconcealed disgust. Even then, with his hand already on the hilt of his sword, he hesitated to draw till a roar, 'En garde, fichtre! What do you think you came here for?' and the rush of his adversary forced him to put himself as quickly as possible in a posture of defence.

The clash of arms filled that prim garden, which hitherto had known no more warlike sound than the click of clipping shears; and presently the upper part of an old lady's body was projected out of a window upstairs. She tossed her arms above her white cap, scolding in a cracked voice. The gardener remained glued to the tree, his toothless mouth open in idiotic astonishment, and a little farther up the path the pretty girl, as if spellbound to a small grass plot, ran a few steps this way and that, wringing her hands and muttering crazily. She did not rush between the combatants: the onslaughts of Lieut. Feraud were so fierce that her heart failed her. Lieut. D'Hubert, his faculties concentrated upon defence, needed all his skill and science of the sword to stop the rushes of his adversary. Twice already he had to break ground. It bothered him to feel his foothold made insecure by the round, dry gravel of the path rolling under the hard soles of his boots. This was most unsuitable ground, he thought, keeping a watchful, narrowed gaze, shaded by long eyelashes, upon the fiery stare of his thick-set adversary. This absurd affair would ruin his reputation of a sensible, well-behaved, promising young officer. It would damage, at any rate, his immediate prospects, and lose him the good-will of his general. These worldly preoccupations were no doubt misplaced in view of the solemnity of the moment. A duel, whether regarded as a ceremony in the cult of honour, or even when reduced in its moral essence to a form of manly sport, demands a perfect singleness of intention, a homicidal austerity of mood. On the other hand, this vivid concern for his future had not a bad effect inasmuch as it began to rouse the anger of Lieut. D'Hubert. Some seventy seconds had elapsed since they had crossed blades, and Lieut. D'Hubert had to break ground again in order to avoid impaling his reckless adversary like a beetle for a cabinet of specimens. The result was that misapprehending the motive, Lieut. Feraud with a triumphant sort of snarl pressed his attack.

'This enraged animal will have me against the wall directly,' thought Lieut. D'Hubert. He imagined himself much closer to the house than he was, and he dared not turn his head; it seemed to him that he was keeping his adversary off with his eyes rather more than with his point. Lieut. Feraud crouched and bounded with a fierce tigerish agility fit to trouble the stoutest heart. But what was more appalling than the fury of a wild beast, accomplishing in all innocence of heart a natural function, was the fixity of savage purpose man alone is capable of displaying. Lieut. D 'Hubert in the midst of his worldly preoccupations perceived it at last. It was an absurd and damaging affair to be drawn into, but whatever silly intention the fellow had started with, it was clear enough that by this time he meant to kill — nothing less. He meant it with an intensity of will utterly beyond the inferior faculties of a tiger.

As is the case with constitutionally brave men, the full view of the danger interested Lieut. D'Hubert. And directly he got properly interested, the length of his arm and the coolness of his head told in his favour. It was the turn of Lieut. Feraud to recoil, with a bloodcurdling grunt of baffled rage. He made a swift feint, and then rushed straight forward.

'Ah! you would, would you?' Lieut. D'Hubert exclaimed, mentally. The combat had lasted nearly two minutes, time enough for any man to get embittered, apart from the merits of the quarrel. And all at once it was over. Trying to close breast to breast under his adversary's guard Lieut. Feraud received a slash on his shortened arm. He did not feel it in the least, but it checked his rush, and his feet slipping on the gravel he fell backwards with great violence. The shock jarred his boiling brain into the perfect quietude of insensibility. Simultaneously with his fall the pretty servant-girl shrieked; but the old maiden lady at the window ceased her scolding, and began to cross herself piously.

Beholding his adversary stretched out perfectly still, his face to the sky, Lieut.

D'Hubert thought he had killed him outright. The impression of having slashed hard enough to cut his man clean in two abode with him for a while in an exaggerated memory of the right good-will he had put into the blow. He dropped on his knees hastily by the side of the prostrate body. Discovering that not even the arm was severed, a slight sense of disappointment mingled with the feeling of relief. The fellow deserved the worst. But truly he did not want the death of that sinner. The affair was ugly enough as it stood, and Lieut. D'Hubert addressed himself at once to the task of stopping the bleeding. In this task it was his fate to be ridiculously impeded by the pretty maid. Rending the air with screams of horror, she attacked him from behind and, twining her fingers in his hair, tugged back at his head. Why she should choose to hinder him at this precise moment he could not in the least understand. He did not try. It was all like a very wicked and harassing dream. Twice to save himself from being pulled over he had to rise and fling her off. He did this stoically, without a word, kneeling down again at once to go on with his work. But the third time, his work being done, he seized her and held her arms pinned to her body. Her cap was half off, her face was red, her eyes blazed with crazy boldness. He looked mildly into them while she called him a wretch, a traitor, and a murderer many times in succession. This did not annoy him so much as the conviction that she had managed to scratch his face abundantly. Ridicule would be added to the scandal of the story. He imagined the adorned tale making its way through the garrison of the town, through the whole army on the frontier, with every possible distortion of motive and sentiment and circumstance, spreading a doubt upon the sanity of his conduct and the distinction of his taste even to the very ears of his honourable family. It was all very well for that fellow Feraud, who had no connections, no family to speak of, and no quality but courage, which, anyhow, was a matter of course, and possessed by every single trooper in the whole mass of French cavalry. Still holding down the arms of the girl in a strong grip, Lieut. D'Hubert glanced over his shoulder. Lieut. Feraud had opened his eyes. He did not move. Like a man just waking from a deep sleep he stared without any expression at the evening sky.

Lieut. D'Hubert's urgent shouts to the old gardener produced no effect — not so much as to make him shut his toothless mouth. Then he remembered that the man was stone deaf. All that time the girl struggled, not with maidenly coyness, but like a pretty, dumb fury, kicking his shins now and then. He continued to hold her as if in a vice, his instinct telling him that were he to let her go she would fly at his eyes. But he was greatly humiliated by his position. At last she gave up. She was more exhausted than appeased, he feared. Nevertheless, he attempted to get out of this wicked dream by way of negotiation.

'Listen to me,' he said, as calmly as he could. 'Will you promise to run for a surgeon if I let you go?'

With real affliction he heard her declare that she would do nothing of the kind. On the contrary, her sobbed out intention was to remain in the garden, and fight tooth and nail for the protection of the vanquished man. This was shocking.

'My dear child!' he cried in despair, 'is it possible that you think me capable of murdering a wounded adversary? Is it . . . Be quiet, you little wild cat, you!'

They struggled. A thick, drowsy voice said behind him, 'What are you after with that girl?'

Lieut. Feraud had raised himself on his good arm. He was looking sleepily at his other arm, at the mess of blood on his uniform, at a small red pool on the ground, at his sabre lying a foot away on the path. Then he laid himself down gently again to think it all out, as far as a thundering headache would permit of mental operations.

Lieut. D'Hubert released the girl who crouched at once by the side of the other lieutenant. The shades of night were falling on the little trim garden with this touching group, whence proceeded low murmurs of sorrow and compassion, with other feeble sounds of a different character, as if an imperfectly awake invalid were trying to swear. Lieut. D'Hubert went away.

He passed through the silent house, and congratulated himself upon the dusk concealing his gory hands and scratched face from the passers-by. But this story could by no means be concealed. He dreaded the discredit and ridicule above everything, and was painfully aware of sneaking through the back streets in the manner of a murderer. Presently the sounds of a flute coming out of the open window of a lighted upstairs room in a modest house interrupted his dismal reflections. It was being played with a persevering virtuosity, and through the fioritures of the tune one could hear the regular thumping of the foot beating time on the floor.

Lieut. D'Hubert shouted a name, which was that of an army surgeon whom he knew

31

fairly well. The sounds of the flute ceased, and the musician appeared at the window, his instrument still in his hand, peering into the street.

'Who calls? You, D'Hubert? What brings you this way?'

He did not like to be disturbed at the hour when he was playing the flute. He was a man whose hair had turned grey already in the thankless task of tying up wounds on battle-fields where others reaped advancement and glory.

'I want you to go at once and see Feraud. You know Lieut. Feraud? He lives down the second street. It's but a step from here.'

'What's the matter with him?'

'Wounded.'

'Are you sure?'

'Sure!' cried D'Hubert. 'I come from there.'

'That's amusing,' said the elderly surgeon. Amusing was his favourite word; but the expression of his face when he pronounced it never corresponded. He was a stolid man. 'Come in,' he added. 'I'll get ready in a moment.'

'Thanks! I will. I want to wash my hands in your room.'

Lieut. D'Hubert found the surgeon occupied in unscrewing his flute, and packing the pieces methodically in a case. He turned his head.

'Water there — in the corner. Your hands do want washing.'

'I've stopped the bleeding,' said Lieut. D'Hubert. 'But you had better make haste. It's rather more than ten minutes ago, you know.'

The surgeon did not hurry his movements.

'What's the matter? Dressing came off? That's amusing. I've been at work in the hospital all day but I've been told this morning by somebody that he had come off without a scratch.'

'Not the same duel probably,' growled moodily Lieut. D'Hubert, wiping his hands on a coarse towel.

'Not the same . . . What? Another. It would take the very devil to make me go out twice in one day.' The surgeon looked narrowly at Lieut. D'Hubert. 'How did you come by that scratched face? Both sides, too — and symmetrical. It's amusing.'

'Very!' snarled Lieut. D'Hubert. 'And you will find his slashed arm amusing, too. It will keep both of you amused for quite a long time.'

The doctor was mystified and impressed by the brusque bitterness of Lieut. D'Hubert's tone. They left the house together, and in the street he was still more mystified by his conduct.

'Aren't you coming with me?' he asked.

'No,' said Lieut. D'Hubert. 'You can find the house by yourself. The front door will be standing open very likely.'

'All right. Where's his room?'

'Ground floor. But you had better go right through and look in the garden first.'

This astonishing piece of information made the surgeon go off without further parley. Lieut. D'Hubert regained his quarters nursing a hot and uneasy indignation. He dreaded the chaff of his comrades almost as much as the anger of his superiors. The truth was confoundedly grotesque and embarrassing, even putting aside the irregularity of the combat itself, which made it come abominably near a criminal offence. Like all men without much imagination, a faculty which helps the process of reflective thought, Lieut. D'Hubert became frightfully harassed by the obvious aspects of his predicament. He was certainly glad that he had not killed Lieut. Feraud outside all rules, and without the regular witnesses proper to such a transaction. Uncommonly glad. At the same time he felt as though he would have liked to wring his neck for him without ceremony.

He was still under the sway of these contradictory sentiments when the surgeon amateur of the flute came to see him. More

34

than three days had elapsed. Lieut. D'Hubert was no longer officier d'ordonnance to the general commanding the division. He had been sent back to his regiment. And he was resuming his connection with the soldiers' military family by being shut up in close confinement, not at his own quarters in town, but in a room in the barracks. Owing to the gravity of the incident, he was forbidden to see any one. He did not know what had happened, what was being said, or what was being thought. The arrival of the surgeon was a most unexpected thing to the worried captive. The amateur of the flute began by explaining that he was there only by a special favour of the colonel.

'I represented to him that it would be only fair to let you have some authentic news of your adversary,' he continued. 'You'll be glad to hear he's getting better fast.'

Lieut. D'Hubert's face exhibited no conventional signs of gladness. He continued to walk the floor of the dusty bare room.

'Take this chair, doctor,' he mumbled.

The doctor sat down.

'This affair is variously appreciated — in town and in the army. In fact, the diversity of opinions is amusing.'

'Is it!' mumbled Lieut. D'Hubert, tramping steadily from wall to wall. But within himself he marvelled that there could be two opinions on the matter. The surgeon continued.

'Of course, as the real facts are not known — '

'I should have thought,' interrupted D'Hubert, 'that the fellow would have put you in possession of facts.'

'He said something,' admitted the other, 'the first time I saw him. And, by the by, I did find him in the garden. The thump on the back of his head had made him a little incoherent then. Afterwards he was rather reticent than otherwise.'

'Didn't think he would have the grace to be ashamed!' mumbled D'Hubert, resuming his pacing while the doctor murmured, 'It's very amusing. Ashamed! Shame was not exactly his frame of mind. However, you may look at the matter otherwise.'

'What are you talking about? What matter?' asked D'Hubert, with a sidelong look at the heavy-faced, grey-haired figure seated on a wooden chair.

'Whatever it is,' said the surgeon a little impatiently, 'I don't want to pronounce any opinion on your conduct — '

'By heavens, you had better not!' burst out D'Hubert.

'There! — there! Don't be so quick in flourishing the sword. It doesn't pay in the long run. Understand once for all that I would not carve any of you youngsters except with the tools of my trade. But my advice is good. If you go on like this you will make for yourself an ugly reputation.'

'Go on like what?' demanded Lieut. D'Hubert, stopping short, quite startled. 'I! — I! — make for myself a reputation . . . What do you imagine?'

'I told you I don't wish to judge of the rights and wrongs of this incident. It's not my business. Nevertheless — '

'What on earth has he been telling you?' interrupted Lieut. D'Hubert, in a sort of awed scare.

'I told you already, that at first, when I picked him up in the garden, he was incoherent. Afterwards he was naturally reticent. But I gather at least that he could not help himself.'

'He couldn't?' shouted Lieut. D'Hubert in a great voice. Then, lowering his tone impressively, 'And what about me? Could I help myself?'

The surgeon stood up. His thoughts were running upon the flute, his constant companion with a consoling voice. In the vicinity of field ambulances, after twenty-four hours' hard work, he had been known to trouble with its sweet sounds the horrible stillness of battlefields, given over to silence and the dead. The solacing hour of his daily life was approaching, and in peace time he held on to the minutes as a miser to his hoard.

'Of course! — of course!' he said, perfunctorily. 'You would think so. It's amusing. However, being perfectly neutral and friendly to you both, I have consented to deliver his message to you. Say that I am humouring an invalid if you like. He wants you to know that this affair is by no means at an end. He intends to send you his seconds directly he has regained his strength — providing, of course, the army is not in the field at that time.'

'He intends, does he? Why, certainly,' spluttered Lieut. D'Hubert in a passion.

The secret of his exasperation was not apparent to the visitor; but this passion confirmed the surgeon in the belief which was gaining ground outside that some very serious difference had arisen between these two young men, something serious enough to wear an air of mystery, some fact of the utmost gravity. To settle their urgent difference about that fact, those two young men had risked being broken and disgraced at the outset almost of their career. The surgeon feared that the forthcoming inquiry would fail to satisfy the public curiosity. They would not take the public into their confidence as to that something which had passed between them of a nature so outrageous as to make them face a charge of murder — neither more nor less. But what could it be?

The surgeon was not very curious by temperament; but that question haunting his mind caused him twice that evening to hold the instrument off his lips and sit silent for a whole minute — right in the middle of a tune — trying to form a plausible conjecture.

2

He succeeded in this object no better than the rest of the garrison and the whole of society. The two young officers, of no especial consequence till then, became distinguished by the universal curiosity as to the origin of their quarrel. Madame de Lionne's salon was the centre of ingenious surmises; that lady herself was for a time assailed by inquiries as being the last person known to have spoken to these unhappy and reckless young men before they went out together from her house to a savage encounter with swords, at dusk, in a private garden. She protested she had not observed anything unusual in their demeanour. Lieut. Feraud had been visibly annoyed at being called away. That was natural enough; no man likes to be disturbed in a conversation with a lady famed for her elegance and sensibility. But in truth the subject bored Madame de Lionne, since her personality could by no stretch of reckless gossip be connected with this affair. And it irritated her to hear it advanced that there might have been some woman in the case. This irritation arose, not from her elegance or sensibility, but from a more instinctive side of her nature. It became so great at last that she peremptorily forbade the subject to be mentioned under her roof. Near her couch the prohibition was obeyed, but farther off in the salon the pall of the imposed silence continued to be lifted more or less. A personage with a long, pale face, resembling the countenance of a sheep, opined, shaking his head, that it was a quarrel of long standing envenomed by time. It was objected to him that the men themselves were too young for such a theory. They belonged also to different and distant parts of France. There were other physical impossibilities, too. A sub-commissary of the Intendence, an agreeable and cultivated bachelor in kerseymere breeches, Hessian boots, and a blue coat embroidered with silver lace, who affected to believe in the transmigration of souls, suggested that the two had met perhaps in some previous existence. The feud was in the forgotten past. It might have been something quite inconceivable in the present state of their being; but their souls remembered the animosity, and manifested an instinctive antagonism. He developed this theme jocularly. Yet the affair was so absurd from the worldly, the military, the honourable, or the prudential point of view, that this weird explanation seemed rather more reasonable than any other.

The two officers had confided nothing definite to any one. Humiliation at having been worsted arms in hand, and an uneasy feeling of having been involved in a scrape by the injustice of fate, kept Lieut. Feraud savagely dumb. He mistrusted the sympathy of mankind. That would, of course, go to that dandified staff officer. Lying in bed, he raved aloud to the pretty maid who administered to his needs with devotion, and listened to his horrible imprecations with alarm. That Lieut. D'Hubert should be made to 'pay for it,' seemed to her just and natural. Her principal care was that Lieut. Feraud should not excite himself. He appeared so wholly admirable and fascinating to the humility of her heart that her only concern was to see him get well quickly, even if it were only to resume his visits to Madame de Lionne's salon.

Lieut. D'Hubert kept silent for the immediate reason that there was no one, except a stupid young soldier servant, to speak to. Further, he was aware that the episode, so grave professionally, had its comic side. When reflecting upon it, he still felt that he would like to wring Lieut. Feraud's neck for him. But this formula was figurative rather than precise, and expressed more a state of mind than an actual physical impulse. At the same time, there was in that young man a

42

feeling of comradeship and kindness which made him unwilling to make the position of Lieut. Feraud worse than it was. He did not want to talk at large about this wretched affair. At the inquiry he would have, of course, to speak the truth in self-defence. This prospect vexed him.

But no inquiry took place. The army took the field instead. Lieut. D'Hubert, liberated without remark, took up his regimental duties; and Lieut. Feraud, his arm just out of the sling, rode unquestioned with his squadron to complete his convalescence in the smoke of battlefields and the fresh air of night bivouacs. This bracing treatment suited him so well, that at the first rumour of an armistice being signed he could turn without misgivings to the thoughts of his private warfare.

This time it was to be regular warfare. He sent two friends to Lieut. D'Hubert, whose regiment was stationed only a few miles away. Those friends had asked no questions of their principal. 'I owe him one, that pretty staff officer,' he had said, grimly, and they went away quite contentedly on their mission. Lieut. D'Hubert had no difficulty in finding two friends equally discreet and devoted to their principal. 'There's a crazy fellow to whom I must give a lesson,' he had declared curtly; and they asked for no better reasons.

On these grounds an encounter with duelling-swords was arranged one early morning in a convenient field. At the third set-to Lieut. D'Hubert found himself lying on his back on the dewy grass with a hole in his side. A serene sun rising over a landscape of meadows and woods hung on his left. A surgeon — not the flute player, but another — was bending over him, feeling around the wound.

'Narrow squeak. But it will be nothing,' he pronounced.

Lieut. D'Hubert heard these words with pleasure. One of his seconds, sitting on the wet grass, and sustaining his head on his lap, said, 'The fortune of war, mon pauvre vieux. What will you have? You had better make it up like two good fellows. Do!'

'You don't know what you ask,' murmured Lieut. D'Hubert, in a feeble voice. 'However, if he . . . '

In another part of the meadow the seconds of Lieut. Feraud were urging him to go over and shake hands with his adversary.

'You have paid him off now — que diable. It's the proper thing to do. This D'Hubert is a decent fellow.'

'I know the decency of these generals' pets,' muttered Lieut. Feraud through his teeth, and the sombre expression of his face discouraged further efforts at reconciliation. The seconds, bowing from a distance, took their men off the field. In the afternoon Lieut. D'Hubert, very popular as a good comrade uniting great bravery with a frank and equable temper, had many visitors. It was remarked that Lieut. Feraud did not, as is customary, show himself much abroad to receive the felicitations of his friends. They would not have failed him, because he, too, was liked for the exuberance of his southern nature and the simplicity of his character. In all the places where officers were in the habit of assembling at the end of the day the duel of the morning was talked over from every point of view. Though Lieut. D'Hubert had got worsted this time, his sword play was commended. No one could deny that it was very close, very scientific. It was even whispered that if he got touched it was because he wished to spare his adversary. But by many the vigour and dash of Lieut. Feraud's attack were pronounced irresistible.

The merits of the two officers as combatants were frankly discussed; but their attitude to each other after the duel was criticised lightly and with caution. It was irreconcilable, and that was to be regretted. But after all they knew best what the care of their honour dictated. It was not a matter for their comrades to pry into over-much. As to the origin of the quarrel, the general impression was that it dated from the time they were holding garrison in Strasbourg. The musical surgeon shook his head at that. It went much farther back, he thought.

'Why, of course! You must know the whole story,' cried several voices, eager with curiosity. 'What was it?'

He raised his eyes from his glass deliberately. 'Even if I knew ever so well, you can't expect me to tell you, since both the principals choose to say nothing.'

He got up and went out, leaving the sense of mystery behind him. He could not stay any longer, because the witching hour of flute-playing was drawing near.

After he had gone a very young officer observed solemnly, 'Obviously, his lips are sealed!'

Nobody questioned the high correctness of that remark. Somehow it added to the impressiveness of the affair. Several older officers of both regiments, prompted by nothing but sheer kindness and love of harmony, proposed to form a Court of Honour, to which the two young men would leave the task of their reconciliation. Unfortunately they began by approaching Lieut. Feraud, on the assumption that, having just scored heavily, he would be found placable and disposed to moderation.

The reasoning was sound enough. Nevertheless, the move turned out unfortunate. In that relaxation of moral fibre, which is brought about by the ease of soothed vanity, Lieut. Feraud had condescended in the secret of his heart to review the case, and even had come to doubt not the justice of his cause, but the absolute sagacity of his conduct. This being so, he was disinclined to talk about it. The suggestion of the regimental wise men put him in a difficult position. He was disgusted at it, and this disgust, by a paradoxical logic, reawakened his animosity against Lieut. D'Hubert. Was he to be pestered with this fellow for ever — the fellow who had an infernal knack of getting round people somehow? And yet it was difficult to refuse point blank that mediation sanctioned by the code of honour.

He met the difficulty by an attitude of grim reserve. He twisted his moustache and used vague words. His case was perfectly clear. He was not ashamed to state it before a proper Court of Honour, neither was he afraid to defend it on the ground. He did not see any reason to jump at the suggestion before ascertaining how his adversary was likely to take it.

Later in the day, his exasperation growing upon him, he was heard in a public place saying sardonically, 'that it would be the very luckiest thing for Lieut. D'Hubert, because the next time of meeting he need not hope to get off with the mere trifle of three weeks in bed.'

This boastful phrase might have been prompted by the most profound Machiavellism. Southern natures often hide, under the outward impulsiveness of action and speech, a certain amount of astuteness.

Lieut. Feraud, mistrusting the justice of men, by no means desired a Court of Honour; and the above words, according so well with his temperament, had also the merit of serving his turn. Whether meant so or not, they found their way in less than four-and-twenty hours into Lieut. D'Hubert's bedroom. In consequence Lieut. D'Hubert, sitting propped up with pillows, received the overtures made to him next day by the statement that the affair was of a nature which could not bear discussion.

The pale face of the wounded officer, his weak voice which he had yet to use cautiously, and the courteous dignity of his tone had a great effect on his hearers. Reported outside all this did more for deepening the mystery than the vapourings of Lieut. Feraud. This last was greatly relieved at the issue. He began to enjoy the state of general wonder, and was pleased to add to it by assuming an attitude of fierce discretion.

The colonel of Lieut. D'Hubert's regiment was a grey-haired, weather-beaten warrior, who took a simple view of his responsibilities. 'I can't,' he said to himself, 'let the best of my subalterns get damaged like this for nothing. I must get to the bottom of this affair privately. He must speak out if the devil were in it. The colonel should be more than a father to these youngsters.' And indeed he loved all his men with as much affection as a father of a large family can feel for every individual member of it. If human beings by an oversight of Providence came into the world as mere civilians, they were born again into a regiment as infants are born into a family, and it was that military birth alone which counted.

At the sight of Lieut. D'Hubert standing before him very bleached and hollow-eyed the heart of the old warrior felt a pang of genuine compassion. All his affection for the regiment — that body of men which he held in his hand to launch forward and draw back, who ministered to his pride and commanded all his thoughts — seemed centred for a moment on the person of the most promising subaltern. He cleared his throat in a threatening manner, and frowned terribly. 'You must understand,' he began, 'that I don't care a rap for the life of a single man in the regiment. I would send the eight hundred and forty-three of you men and horses galloping into the pit of perdition with no more compunction than I would kill a fly!'

'Yes, Colonel. You would be riding at our head,' said Lieut. D'Hubert with a wan smile.

The colonel, who felt the need of being very diplomatic, fairly roared at this. 'I want you to know, Lieut. D'Hubert, that I could stand aside and see you all riding to Hades if need be. I am a man to do even that if the good of the service and my duty to my country required it from me. But that's unthinkable, so don't you even hint at such a thing.' He glared awfully, but his tone softened. 'There's some milk yet about that moustache of yours, my boy. You don't know what a man like me is capable of. I would hide behind a haystack if . . . Don't grin at me, sir! How dare you? If this were not a private conversation I would . . . Look here! I am responsible for the proper expenditure of lives under my command for the glory of our country and the honour of the regiment. Do you understand that? Well, then, what the devil do you mean by letting yourself be spitted like this by that fellow of the 7th Hussars? It's simply disgraceful!'

Lieut. D'Hubert felt vexed beyond measure. His shoulders moved slightly. He made no other answer. He could not ignore his responsibility.

The colonel veiled his glance and lowered his voice still more. 'It's deplorable!' he murmured. And again he changed his tone. 'Come!' he went on, persuasively, but with that note of authority which dwells in the throat of a good leader of men, 'this affair must be settled. I desire to be told plainly what it is all about. I demand, as your best friend, to know.'

The compelling power of authority, the persuasive influence of kindness, affected powerfully a man just risen from a bed of sickness. Lieut. D'Hubert's hand, which grasped the knob of a stick, trembled slightly. But his northern temperament, sentimental yet cautious and clear-sighted, too, in its idealistic way, checked his impulse to make a clean breast of the whole deadly absurdity. According to the precept of transcendental wisdom, he turned his tongue seven times in his mouth before he spoke. He made then only a speech of thanks.

The colonel listened, interested at first, then looked mystified. At last he frowned. 'You hesitate? — mille tonnerres! Haven't I told you that I will condescend to argue with you — as a friend?'

'Yes, Colonel!' answered Lieut. D'Hubert, gently. 'But I am afraid that after you have heard me out as a friend you will take action as my superior officer.'

The attentive colonel snapped his jaws. 'Well, what of that?' he said, frankly. 'Is it so damnably disgraceful?'

'It is not,' negatived Lieut. D'Hubert, in a faint but firm voice.

'Of course, I shall act for the good of the service. Nothing can prevent me doing that. What do you think I want to be told for?'

'I know it is not from idle curiosity,' protested Lieut. D'Hubert. 'I know you will act wisely. But what about the good fame of the regiment?'

'It cannot be affected by any youthful folly of a lieutenant,' said the colonel, severely.

'No. It cannot be. But it can be by evil tongues. It will be said that a lieutenant of the 4th Hussars, afraid of meeting his adversary, is hiding behind his colonel. And that would be worse than hiding behind a haystack — for the good of the service. I cannot afford to do that, Colonel.'

'Nobody would dare to say anything of the kind,' began the colonel very fiercely, but ended the phrase on an uncertain note. The bravery of Lieut. D'Hubert was well known. But the colonel was well aware that the duelling courage, the single combat courage, is rightly or wrongly supposed to be courage of a special sort. And it was eminently necessary that an officer of his regiment should possess every kind of courage — and prove it, too. The colonel stuck out his lower lip, and looked far away with a peculiar glazed stare. This was the expression of his perplexity — an expression practically unknown to his regiment; for perplexity is a sentiment which is incompatible with the rank of colonel of cavalry. The colonel himself was overcome by the unpleasant novelty of the sensation. As he was not accustomed to think except on professional matters connected with the welfare of men and horses, and the proper use thereof on the field of glory, his intellectual efforts degenerated into mere mental repetitions of profane language. 'Mille tonnerres! . . . Sacre nom de nom . . . ' he thought.

Lieut. D'Hubert coughed painfully, and added in a weary voice: 'There will be plenty of evil tongues to say that I've been cowed. And I am sure you will not expect me to pass that over. I may find myself suddenly with a dozen duels on my hands instead of this one affair.'

The direct simplicity of this argument

came home to the colonel's understanding. He looked at his subordinate fixedly. 'Sit down, Lieutenant!' he said, gruffly. 'This is the very devil of a . . . Sit down!'

'Mon Colonel,' D'Hubert began again, 'I am not afraid of evil tongues. There's a way of silencing them. But there's my peace of mind, too. I wouldn't be able to shake off the notion that I've ruined a brother officer. Whatever action you take, it is bound to go farther. The inquiry has been dropped — let it rest now. It would have been absolutely fatal to Feraud.'

'Hey! What! Did he behave so badly?'

'Yes. It was pretty bad,' muttered Lieut. D'Hubert. Being still very weak, he felt a disposition to cry.

As the other man did not belong to his own regiment the colonel had no difficulty in believing this. He began to pace up and down the room. He was a good chief, a man capable of discreet sympathy. But he was human in other ways, too, and this became apparent because he was not capable of artifice.

'The very devil, Lieutenant,' he blurted out, in the innocence of his heart, 'is that I have declared my intention to get to the bottom of this affair. And when a colonel says something . . . you see . . . '

Lieut. D'Hubert broke in earnestly: 'Let

me entreat you, Colonel, to be satisfied with taking my word of honour that I was put into a damnable position where I had no option; I had no choice whatever, consistent with my dignity as a man and an officer . . . After all, Colonel, this fact is the very bottom of this affair. Here you've got it. The rest is mere detail . . . '

The colonel stopped short. The reputation of Lieut. D'Hubert for good sense and good temper weighed in the balance. A cool head, a warm heart, open as the day. Always correct in his behaviour. One had to trust him. The colonel repressed manfully an immense curiosity. 'H'm! You affirm that as a man and an officer . . . No option? Eh?'

'As an officer — an officer of the 4th Hussars, too,' insisted Lieut. D'Hubert, 'I had not. And that is the bottom of the affair, Colonel.'

'Yes. But still I don't see why, to one's colonel . . . A colonel is a father — que diable!'

Lieut. D'Hubert ought not to have been allowed out as yet. He was becoming aware of his physical insufficiency with humiliation and despair. But the morbid obstinacy of an invalid possessed him, and at the same time he felt with dismay his eyes filling with water. This trouble seemed too big to handle. A tear fell down the thin, pale cheek of Lieut. D'Hubert.

The colonel turned his back on him hastily. You could have heard a pin drop. 'This is some silly woman story — is it not?'

Saying these words the chief spun round to seize the truth, which is not a beautiful shape living in a well, but a shy bird best caught by stratagem. This was the last move of the colonel's diplomacy. He saw the truth shining unmistakably in the gesture of Lieut. D'Hubert raising his weak arms and his eyes to heaven in supreme protest.

'Not a woman affair — eh?' growled the colonel, staring hard. 'I don't ask you who or where. All I want to know is whether there is a woman in it?'

Lieut. D'Hubert's arms dropped, and his weak voice was pathetically broken.

'Nothing of the kind, mon Colonel.'

'On your honour?' insisted the old warrior.

'On my honour.'

'Very well,' said the colonel, thoughtfully, and bit his lip. The arguments of Lieut. D'Hubert, helped by his liking for the man, had convinced him. On the other hand, it was highly improper that his intervention, of which he had made no secret, should produce no visible effect. He kept Lieut. D'Hubert a few minutes longer, and dismissed him kindly.

'Take a few days more in bed. Lieutenant. What the devil does the surgeon mean by reporting you fit for duty?'

On coming out of the colonel's quarters, Lieut. D'Hubert said nothing to the friend who was waiting outside to take him home. He said nothing to anybody. Lieut. D'Hubert made no confidences. But on the evening of that day the colonel, strolling under the elms growing near his quarters, in the company of his second in command, opened his lips.

'I've got to the bottom of this affair,' he remarked. The lieut.-colonel, a dry, brown chip of a man with short side-whiskers, pricked up his ears at that without letting a sign of curiosity escape him.

'It's no trifle,' added the colonel, oracularly. The other waited for a long while before he murmured:

'Indeed, sir!'

'No trifle,' repeated the colonel, looking straight before him. 'I've, however, forbidden D'Hubert either to send to or receive a challenge from Feraud for the next twelve months.'

He had imagined this prohibition to save the prestige a colonel should have. The result of it was to give an official seal to the mystery surrounding this deadly quarrel. Lieut. D'Hubert repelled by an impassive silence all attempts to worm the truth out of him. Lieut. Feraud, secretly uneasy at first, regained his assurance as time went on. He disguised his ignorance of the meaning of the imposed truce by slight sardonic laughs, as though he were amused by what he intended to keep to himself. 'But what will you do?' his chums used to ask him. He contented himself by replying 'Qui vivra verra' with a little truculent air. And everybody admired his discretion.

Before the end of the truce Lieut. D'Hubert got his troop. The promotion was well earned, but somehow no one seemed to expect the event. When Lieut. Feraud heard of it at a gathering of officers, he muttered through his teeth, 'Is that so?' At once he unhooked his sabre from a peg near the door, buckled it on carefully, and left the company without another word. He walked home with measured steps, struck a light with his flint and steel, and lit his tallow candle. Then snatching an unlucky glass tumbler off the mantelpiece he dashed it violently on the floor.

Now that D'Hubert was an officer of superior rank there could be no question of a duel. Neither of them could send or receive a challenge without rendering himself amenable to a court-martial. It was not to be thought of. Lieut. Feraud, who for many days now had experienced no real desire to meet Lieut. D'Hubert arms in hand, chafed again at the systematic injustice of fate. 'Does he think he will escape me in that way?' he thought, indignantly. He saw in this promotion an intrigue, a conspiracy, a cowardly manoeuvre. That colonel knew what he was doing. He had hastened to recommend his favourite for a step. It was outrageous that a man should be able to avoid the consequences of his acts in such a dark and tortuous manner.

Of a happy-go-lucky disposition, of a temperament more pugnacious than military, Lieut. Feraud had been content to give and receive blows for sheer love of armed strife, and without much thought of advancement; but now an urgent desire to get on sprang up in his breast. This fighter by vocation resolved in his mind to seize showy occasions and to court the favourable opinion of his chiefs like a mere worldling. He knew he was as brave as any one, and never doubted his personal charm. Nevertheless, neither the bravery nor the charm seemed to work very swiftly. Lieut. Feraud's engaging, careless truculence of a beau sabreur underwent a change. He began to make bitter allusions to 'clever fellows who stick at nothing to get on.' The army was full of them, he would say; you had only to look round. But all the time he had in view one person only, his adversary, D'Hubert. Once he confided to an appreciative friend: 'You see, I don't know how to fawn on the right sort of people. It isn't in my character.'

He did not get his step till a week after Austerlitz. The Light Cavalry of the Grand Army had its hands very full of interesting work for a little while. Directly the pressure of professional occupation had been eased Captain Feraud took measures to arrange a meeting without loss of time. 'I know my bird,' he observed, grimly. 'If I don't look sharp he will take care to get himself promoted over the heads of a dozen better men than himself. He's got the knack for that sort of thing.'

This duel was fought in Silesia. If not fought to a finish, it was, at any rate, fought to a standstill. The weapon was the cavalry sabre, and the skill, the science, the vigour, and the determination displayed by the adversaries compelled the admiration of the beholders. It became the subject of talk on both shores of the Danube, and as far as the garrisons of Gratz and Laybach. They crossed blades seven times. Both had many cuts which bled profusely. Both refused to have the combat stopped, time after time, with what appeared the most deadly animosity. This appearance was caused on the part of Captain D'Hubert by a rational desire to be done once for all with this worry; on the part of Captain Feraud by a tremendous exaltation of his pugnacious instincts and the incitement of wounded vanity. At last, dishevelled, their shirts in rags, covered with gore and hardly able to stand, they were led away forcibly by their marvelling and horrified seconds. Later on, besieged by comrades avid of details, these gentlemen declared that they could not have allowed that sort of hacking to go on indefinitely. Asked whether the quarrel was settled this time, they gave it out as their conviction that it was a difference which could only be settled by one of the parties remaining lifeless on the ground. The sensation spread from army corps to army corps, and penetrated at last to the smallest detachments of the troops cantoned between the Rhine and the Save. In the cafes in Vienna it was generally estimated, from details to hand, that the adversaries would be able to meet again in three weeks' time on the outside. Something really transcendent in the way of duelling was expected.

These expectations were brought to naught by the necessities of the service which separated the two officers. No official notice had been taken of their quarrel. It was now the property of the army, and not to be meddled with lightly. But the story of the duel, or rather their duelling propensities, must have stood somewhat in the way of their advancement, because they were still captains when they came together again during the war with Prussia. Detached north after Jena, with the army commanded by Marshal Bernadotte, Prince of Ponte Corvo, they entered Lubeck together.

It was only after the occupation of that town that Captain Feraud found leisure to consider his future conduct in view of the fact that Captain D'Hubert had been given the position of third aide-de-camp to the marshal. He considered it a great part of a night, and in the morning summoned two sympathetic friends.

'I've been thinking it over calmly,' he said, gazing at them with blood-shot, tired eyes. 'I see that I must get rid of that intriguing personage. Here he's managed to sneak on to the personal staff of the marshal. It's a direct provocation to me. I can't tolerate a situation in which I am exposed any day to receive an order through him. And God knows what order, too! That sort of thing has happened once before — and that's once too often. He understands this perfectly, never fear. I can't tell you any more. Now you know what it is you have to do.'

This encounter took place outside the town of Lubeck, on very open ground, selected with special care in deference to the general sentiment of the cavalry division belonging to the army corps, that this time the two officers should meet on horseback. After all, this duel was a cavalry affair, and to persist in fighting on foot would look like a slight on one's own arm of the service. The seconds, startled by the unusual nature of the suggestion, hastened to refer to their principals. Captain Feraud jumped at it with alacrity. For some obscure reason, depending, no doubt, on his psychology, he imagined himself invincible on horseback. All alone within the four walls of his room he rubbed his hands and muttered triumphantly, 'Aha! my pretty staff officer, I've got you now.'

Captain D'Hubert on his side, after staring hard for a considerable time at his friends, shrugged his shoulders slightly. This affair had hopelessly and unreasonably complicated his existence for him. One absurdity more or less in the development did not matter — all absurdity was distasteful to him; but, urbane as ever, he produced a faintly ironical smile, and said in his calm voice, 'It certainly will do away to some extent with the monotony of the thing.'

When left alone, he sat down at a table and took his head into his hands. He had not spared himself of late and the marshal had been working all his aides-de-camp particularly hard. The last three weeks of campaigning in horrible weather had affected his health. When over-tired he suffered from a stitch in his wounded side, and that uncomfortable sensation always depressed him. 'It's that brute's doing, too,' he thought bitterly.

The day before he had received a letter from home, announcing that his only sister was going to be married. He reflected that from the time she was nineteen and he twenty-six, when he went away to garrison life in Strasbourg, he had had but two short glimpses of her. They had been great friends and confidants; and now she was going to be given away to a man whom he did not know — a very worthy fellow no doubt, but not half good enough for her. He would never see his old Leonie again. She had a capable little head, and plenty of tact; she would know how to manage the fellow, to be sure. He was easy in his mind about her happiness but he felt ousted from the first place in her thoughts which had been his ever since the girl could speak. A melancholy regret of the days of his childhood settled upon Captain D'Hubert, third aide-de-camp to the Prince of Ponte Corvo.

He threw aside the letter of congratulation he had begun to write as in duty bound, but without enthusiasm. He took a fresh piece of paper, and traced on it the words: 'This is my last will and testament.' Looking at these words he gave himself up to unpleasant reflection; a presentiment that he would never see the scenes of his childhood weighed down the equable spirits of Captain D'Hubert. He jumped up, pushing his chair back, yawned elaborately in sign that he didn't care anything for presentiments, and throwing himself on the bed went to sleep. During the night he shivered from time to time without waking up. In the morning he rode out of town between his two seconds, talking of indifferent things, and looking right and left with apparent detachment into the heavy morning mists shrouding the flat green fields bordered by hedges. He leaped a ditch, and saw the forms of many mounted men moving in the fog. 'We are to fight before a gallery, it seems,' he muttered to himself, bitterly.

His seconds were rather concerned at the state of the atmosphere, but presently a pale, sickly sun struggled out of the low vapours, and Captain D'Hubert made out, in the distance, three horsemen riding a little apart from the others. It was Captain Feraud and his seconds. He drew his sabre, and assured himself that it was properly fastened to his wrist. And now the seconds, who had been standing in close group with the heads of their horses together, separated at an easy canter, leaving a large, clear field between him and his adversary. Captain D'Hubert looked at the pale sun, at the dismal fields, and the imbecility of the impending fight filled him with desolation. From a distant part of the field a stentorian voice shouted commands at proper intervals: Au pas — Au trot — Charrrgez! . . . Presentiments of death don't come to a man for nothing, he thought at the very moment he put spurs to his horse.

And therefore he was more than surprised when, at the very first set-to, Captain Feraud laid himself open to a cut over the forehead, which blinding him with blood, ended the combat almost before it had fairly begun. It was impossible to go on. Captain D'Hubert, leaving his enemy swearing horribly and reeling in the saddle between his two appalled friends, leaped the ditch again into the road and trotted home with his two seconds, who seemed rather awestruck at the speedy issue of that encounter. In the evening Captain D'Hubert finished the congratulatory letter on his sister's marriage.

He finished it late. It was a long letter. Captain D'Hubert gave reins to his fancy. He told his sister that he would feel rather lonely after this great change in her life; but then the day would come for him, too, to get married. In fact, he was thinking already of the time when there would be no one left to fight with in Europe and the epoch of wars would be over. 'I expect then,' he wrote, 'to be within measurable distance of a marshal's baton, and you will be an experienced married woman. You shall look out a wife for me. I will be, probably, bald by then, and a little blase. I shall require a young girl, pretty of course, and with a large fortune, which should help me to close my glorious career in the splendour befitting my exalted rank.' He ended with the information that he had just given a lesson to a worrying, quarrelsome fellow who imagined he had a grievance against him. 'But if you, in the depths of your province,' he continued, 'ever hear it said that your brother is of a quarrelsome disposition, don't you believe it on any account. There is no saying what gossip from the army may reach your innocent ears. Whatever you hear you may rest assured that your ever-loving brother is not a duellist.' Then Captain D'Hubert crumpled up the blank sheet of paper headed with the words 'This is my last will and testament,' and threw it in the fire with a great laugh at himself. He didn't care a snap for what that lunatic could do. He had suddenly acquired the conviction that his adversary was utterly powerless to affect his life in any sort of way; except, perhaps, in the way of putting a special excitement into the delightful, gay intervals between the campaigns.

From this on there were, however, to be no peaceful intervals in the career of Captain D'Hubert. He saw the fields of Eylau and Friedland, marched and countermarched in the snow, in the mud, in the dust of Polish plains, picking up distinction and advancement on all the roads of North-eastern Europe. Meantime, Captain Feraud, despatched southwards with his regiment, made unsatisfactory war in Spain. It was only when the preparations for the Russian campaign began that he was ordered north again. He left the country of mantillas and oranges without regret.

The first signs of a not unbecoming baldness added to the lofty aspect of Colonel D'Hubert's forehead. This feature was no longer white and smooth as in the days of his youth; the kindly open glance of his blue eyes had grown a little hard as if from much peering through the smoke of battles. The ebony crop on Colonel Feraud's head, coarse and crinkly like a cap of horsehair, showed many silver threads about the temples. A detestable warfare of ambushes and inglorious surprises had not improved his temper. The beak-like curve of his nose was unpleasantly set off by a deep fold on each side of his mouth. The round orbits of his eyes radiated wrinkles. More than ever he recalled an irritable and staring bird — something like a cross between a parrot and an owl. He was still extremely outspoken in his dislike of 'intriguing fellows.' He seized every opportunity to state that he did not pick up his rank in the ante-rooms of marshals. The unlucky persons, civil or military, who, with an intention of being pleasant, begged Colonel Feraud to tell them how he came by that very apparent scar on the forehead, were astonished to find themselves snubbed in various ways, some of which were simply rude and others mysteriously sardonic. Young officers were warned kindly by their more experienced comrades not to stare openly at the colonel's scar. But indeed an officer need have been very young in his profession not to have heard the legendary tale of that duel originating in a mysterious, unforgivable offence.

3

The retreat from Moscow submerged all private feelings in a sea of disaster and misery. Colonels without regiments, D'Hubert and Feraud carried the musket in the ranks of the so-called sacred battalion — a battalion recruited from officers of all arms who had no longer any troops to lead.

In that battalion promoted colonels did duty as sergeants; the generals captained the companies; a marshal of France, Prince of the Empire, commanded the whole. All had provided themselves with muskets picked up on the road, and with cartridges taken from the dead. In the general destruction of the bonds of discipline and duty holding together the companies, the battalions, the regiments, the brigades, and divisions of an armed host, this body of men put its pride in preserving some semblance of order and formation. The only stragglers were those who fell out to give up to the frost their exhausted souls. They plodded on, and their passage did not disturb the mortal silence of the plains, shining with the livid light of snows under a sky the colour of ashes. Whirlwinds ran along the fields, broke against the dark column, enveloped it in a turmoil of flying icicles, and subsided, disclosing it creeping on its tragic way without the swing and rhythm of the military pace. It struggled onwards, the men exchanging neither words nor looks; whole ranks marched touching elbow, day after day and never raising their eyes from the ground, as if lost in despairing reflections. In the dumb, black forests of pines the cracking of overloaded branches was the only sound they heard. Often from daybreak to dusk no one spoke in the whole column. It was like a macabre march of struggling corpses towards a distant grave. Only an alarm of Cossacks could restore to their eyes a semblance of martial resolution. The battalion faced about and deployed, or formed square under the endless fluttering of snowflakes. A cloud of horsemen with fur caps on their heads, levelled long lances, and yelled 'Hurrah! Hurrah!' around their menacing immobility whence, with muffled detonations, hundreds of dark red flames darted through the air thick with falling snow. In a very few moments the horsemen would disappear, as if carried off yelling in the gale, and the sacred battalion standing still, alone in the blizzard, heard only the howling of the wind, whose blasts searched their very hearts. Then, with a cry or two of 'Vive l'Empereur!' it would resume its march, leaving behind a few lifeless bodies lying huddled up, tiny black specks on the white immensity of the snows.

Though often marching in the ranks, or skirmishing in the woods side by side, the two officers ignored each other; this not so much from inimical intention as from a very real indifference. All their store of moral energy was expended in resisting the terrific enmity of nature and the crushing sense of irretrievable disaster. To the last they counted among the most active, the least demoralized of the battalion; their vigorous vitality invested them both with the appearance of an heroic pair in the eyes of their comrades. And they never exchanged more than a casual word or two, except one day, when skirmishing in front of the battalion against a worrying attack of cavalry, they found themselves cut off in the woods by a small party of Cossacks. A score of fur-capped, hairy horsemen rode to and fro, brandishing their lances in ominous silence; but the two officers had no mind to lay down their arms, and Colonel Feraud suddenly spoke up in a hoarse, growling voice, bringing his firelock to the shoulder. 'You take the nearest brute, Colonel D'Hubert; I'll settle the next one. I am a better shot than you are.'

Colonel D'Hubert nodded over his levelled musket. Their shoulders were pressed against the trunk of a large tree; on their front enormous snowdrifts protected them from a direct charge. Two carefully aimed shots rang out in the frosty air, two Cossacks reeled in their saddles. The rest, not thinking the game good enough, closed round their wounded comrades and galloped away out of range. The two officers managed to rejoin their battalion halted for the night. During that afternoon they had leaned upon each other more than once, and towards the end, Colonel D'Hubert, whose long legs gave him an advantage in walking through soft snow, peremptorily took the musket of Colonel Feraud from him and carried it on his shoulder, using his own as a staff.

On the outskirts of a village half buried in the snow an old wooden barn burned with a clear and an immense flame. The sacred battalion of skeletons, muffled in rags, crowded greedily the windward side, stretching hundreds of numbed, bony hands to the blaze. Nobody had noted their approach. Before entering the circle of light playing on the sunken, glassy-eyed, starved faces, Colonel D'Hubert spoke in his turn:

'Here's your musket, Colonel Feraud. I can walk better than you.'

Colonel Feraud nodded, and pushed on towards the warmth of the fierce flames. Colonel D'Hubert was more deliberate, but not the less bent on getting a place in the front rank. Those they shouldered aside tried to greet with a faint cheer the reappearance of the two indomitable companions in activity and endurance. Those manly qualities had never perhaps received a higher tribute than this feeble acclamation.

This is the faithful record of speeches exchanged during the retreat from Moscow by Colonels Feraud and D'Hubert. Colonel Feraud's taciturnity was the outcome of concentrated rage. Short, hairy, black faced, with layers of grime and the thick sprouting of a wiry beard, a frost-bitten hand wrapped up in filthy rags carried in a sling, he accused fate of unparalleled perfidy towards the sublime Man of Destiny. Colonel D'Hubert, his long moustaches pendent in icicles on each side of his cracked blue lips, his eyelids inflamed with the glare of snows, the principal part of his costume consisting of a sheepskin coat looted with difficulty from the frozen corpse of a camp follower found in an abandoned cart, took a more thoughtful view of events. His regularly handsome features, now reduced to mere bony lines and fleshless hollows, looked out of a woman's black velvet hood, over which was rammed forcibly a cocked hat picked up under the wheels of an empty army fourgon, which must have contained at one time some general officer's luggage. The sheepskin coat being short for a man of his inches ended very high up, and the skin of his legs, blue with the cold, showed through the tatters of his nether garments. This under the circumstances provoked neither jeers nor pity. No one cared how the next man felt or looked. Colonel D'Hubert himself, hardened to exposure, suffered mainly in his self-respect from the lamentable indecency of his costume. A thoughtless person may think that with a whole host of inanimate bodies bestrewing the path of retreat there could not have been much difficulty in supplying the deficiency. But to loot a pair of breeches from a frozen corpse is not so easy as it may appear to a mere theorist. It requires time and labour. You must remain behind while your companions march on. Colonel D'Hubert had his scruples as to falling out. Once he had stepped aside he could not be sure of ever rejoining his battalion; and the ghastly intimacy of a wrestling match with the frozen dead opposing the unyielding rigidity of iron to your violence was repugnant to the delicacy of his feelings. Luckily, one day, grubbing in a mound of snow between the huts of a village in the hope of finding there a frozen potato or some vegetable garbage he could put between his long and shaky teeth, Colonel D'Hubert uncovered a couple of mats of the sort Russian peasants use to line the sides of their carts with. These, beaten free of frozen snow, bent about his elegant person and fastened solidly round his waist, made a bell-shaped nether garment, a sort of stiff petticoat, which rendered Colonel D'Hubert a perfectly decent, but a much more noticeable figure than before.

Thus accoutred, he continued to retreat, never doubting of his personal escape, but full of other misgivings. The early buoyancy of his belief in the future was destroyed. If the road of glory led through such unforeseen passages, he asked himself — for he was reflective — whether the guide was altogether trustworthy. It was a patriotic sadness, not unmingled with some personal concern, and quite unlike the unreasoning indignation against men and things nursed by Colonel Feraud. Recruiting his strength in a little German town for three weeks, Colonel D'Hubert was surprised to discover within himself a love of repose. His returning vigour was strangely pacific in its aspirations. He meditated silently upon this bizarre change of mood. No doubt many of his brother officers of field rank went through the same moral experience. But these were not the times to talk of it. In one of his letters home Colonel D'Hubert wrote, 'All your plans, my dear Leonie, for marrying me to the charming girl you have discovered in your neighbourhood, seem farther off than ever. Peace is not yet. Europe wants another lesson. It will be a hard task for us, but it shall be done, because the Emperor is invincible.'

Thus wrote Colonel D'Hubert from Pomerania to his married sister Leonie, settled in the south of France. And so far the sentiments expressed would not have been disowned by Colonel Feraud, who wrote no letters to anybody, whose father had been in life an illiterate blacksmith, who had no sister or brother, and whom no one desired ardently to pair off for a life of peace with a charming young girl. But Colonel D'Hubert's letter contained also some philosophical generalities upon the uncertainty of all personal hopes, when bound up entirely with the prestigious fortune of one incomparably great it is true, yet still remaining but a man in his greatness. This view would have appeared rank heresy to Colonel Feraud. Some melancholy forebodings of a military kind, expressed cautiously, would have been pronounced as nothing short of high treason by Colonel Feraud. But Leonie, the sister of Colonel D'Hubert, read them with profound satisfaction, and, folding the letter thoughtfully, remarked to herself that 'Armand was likely to prove eventually a sensible fellow.' Since her marriage into a Southern family she had become a convinced believer in the return of the legitimate king. Hopeful and anxious she offered prayers night and morning, and burnt candles in churches for the safety and prosperity of her brother.

She had every reason to suppose that her prayers were heard. Colonel D'Hubert passed through Lutzen, Bautzen, and Leipsic losing no limb, and acquiring additional reputation. Adapting his conduct to the needs of that desperate time, he had never voiced his misgivings. He concealed them under a cheerful courtesy of such pleasant character that people were inclined to ask themselves with wonder whether Colonel D'Hubert was aware of any disasters. Not only his manners, but even his glances remained untroubled. The steady amenity of his blue eyes disconcerted all grumblers, and made despair itself pause.

This bearing was remarked favourably by the Emperor himself; for Colonel D'Hubert, attached now to the Major-General's staff, came on several occasions under the imperial eye. But it exasperated the higher strung nature of Colonel Feraud. Passing through Magdeburg on service, this last allowed himself, while seated gloomily at dinner with the Commandant de Place, to say of his life-long adversary: 'This man does not love the Emperor,' and his words were received by the other guests in profound silence. Colonel Feraud, troubled in his conscience at the atrocity of the aspersion, felt the need to back it up by a good argument. 'I ought to know him,' he cried, adding some oaths. 'One studies one's adversary. I have met him on the ground half a dozen times, as all the army knows. What more do you want? If that isn't opportunity enough for any fool to size up his man, may the devil take me if I can tell what is.' And he looked around the table, obstinate and sombre.

Later on in Paris, while extremely busy reorganizing his regiment, Colonel Feraud learned that Colonel D'Hubert had been made a general. He glared at his informant incredulously, then folded his arms and turned away muttering, 'Nothing surprises me on the part of that man.'

And aloud he added, speaking over his shoulder, 'You would oblige me greatly by telling General D'Hubert at the first opportunity that his advancement saves him for a time from a pretty hot encounter. I was only waiting for him to turn up here.'

The other officer remonstrated.

'Could you think of it, Colonel Feraud, at this time, when every life should be consecrated to the glory and safety of France?'

But the strain of unhappiness caused by military reverses had spoiled Colonel Feraud's character. Like many other men, he was rendered wicked by misfortune.

'I cannot consider General D'Hubert's existence of any account either for the glory or safety of France,' he snapped viciously. 'You don't pretend, perhaps, to know him better than I do — I who have met him half a dozen times on the ground — do you?'

His interlocutor, a young man, was silenced. Colonel Feraud walked up and down the room.

'This is not the time to mince matters,' he said. 'I can't believe that that man ever loved the Emperor. He picked up his general's stars under the boots of Marshal Berthier. Very well. I'll get mine in another fashion, and then we shall settle this business which has been dragging on too long.'

General D'Hubert, informed indirectly of Colonel Feraud's attitude, made a gesture as if to put aside an importunate person. His thoughts were solicited by graver cares. He had had no time to go and see his family. His sister, whose royalist hopes were rising higher every day, though proud of her brother, regretted his recent advancement in a measure, because it put on him a prominent mark of the usurper's favour, which later on could have an adverse influence upon his career. He wrote to her that no one but an inveterate enemy could say he had got his promotion by favour. As to his career, he assured her that he looked no farther forward into the future than the next battlefield.

Beginning the campaign of France in this dogged spirit, General D'Hubert was wounded on the second day of the battle under Laon. While being carried off the field he heard that Colonel Feraud, promoted this moment to general, had been sent to replace him at the head of his brigade. He cursed his luck impulsively, not being able at the first glance to discern all the advantages of a nasty wound. And yet it was by this heroic method that Providence was shaping his future. Travelling slowly south to his sister's country home under the care of a trusty old servant, General D'Hubert was spared the humiliating contacts and the perplexities of conduct which assailed the men of Napoleonic empire at the moment of its downfall. Lying in his bed, with the windows of his room open wide to the sunshine of Provence, he perceived the undisguised aspect of the blessing conveyed by that jagged fragment of a Prussian shell, which, killing his horse and ripping open his thigh, saved him from an active conflict with his conscience. After the last fourteen years spent sword in hand in the saddle, and with the sense of his duty done to the very end, General D'Hubert found resignation an easy virtue. His sister was delighted with his reasonableness. 'I leave myself altogether in your hands, my dear Leonie,' he had said to her.

He was still laid up when, the credit of his brother-in-law's family being exerted on his behalf, he received from the royal government not only the confirmation of his rank, but the assurance of being retained on the active list. To this was added an unlimited convalescent leave. The unfavourable opinion entertained of him in Bonapartist circles, though it rested on nothing more solid than the unsupported pronouncement of General Feraud, was directly responsible for General D'Hubert's retention on the active list. As to General Feraud, his rank was confirmed, too. It was more than he dared to expect; but Marshal Soult, then Minister of War to the restored king, was partial to officers who had served in Spain. Only not even the marshal's protection could secure for him active employment. He remained irreconcilable, idle, and sinister. He sought in obscure restaurants the company of other half-pay officers who cherished dingy but glorious old tricolour cockades in their breast-pockets, and buttoned with the forbidden eagle buttons their shabby uniforms, declaring themselves too poor to afford the expense of the prescribed change.

The triumphant return from Elba, an historical fact as marvellous and incredible as the exploits of some mythological demi-god, found General D'Hubert still quite unable to sit a horse. Neither could he walk very well. These disabilities, which Madame Leonie accounted most lucky, helped to keep her brother out of all possible mischief. His frame of mind at that time, she noted with dismay, became very far from reasonable. This general officer, still menaced by the loss of a limb, was discovered one night in the stables of the chateau by a groom, who, seeing a light, raised an alarm of thieves. His crutch was lying half-buried in the straw of the litter, and the general was hopping on one leg in a loose box around a snorting horse he was trying to saddle. Such were the effects of imperial magic upon a calm temperament and a pondered mind. Beset in the light of stable lanterns, by the tears, entreaties, indignation, remonstrances and reproaches of his family, he got out of the difficult situation by fainting away there and then in the arms of his nearest relatives, and was carried off to bed. Before he got out of it again, the second reign of Napoleon, the Hundred Days of feverish agitation and supreme effort, passed away like a terrifying dream. The tragic year 1815, begun in the trouble and unrest of consciences, was ending in vengeful proscriptions.

How General Feraud escaped the clutches of the Special Commission and the last offices of a firing squad he never knew himself. It was partly due to the subordinate position he was assigned during the Hundred Days. The Emperor had never given him active command, but had kept him busy at the cavalry depot in Paris, mounting and despatching hastily drilled troopers into the field. Considering this task as unworthy of his abilities, he had discharged it with no offensively noticeable zeal; but for the greater part he was saved from the excesses of Royalist reaction by the interference of General D'Hubert.

This last, still on convalescent leave, but able now to travel, had been despatched by his sister to Paris to present himself to his legitimate sovereign. As no one in the capital could possibly know anything of the episode in the stable he was received there with distinction. Military to the very bottom of his soul, the prospect of rising in his profession consoled him from finding himself the butt of Bonapartist malevolence, which pursued him with a persistence he could not account for. All the rancour of that embittered and persecuted party pointed to him as the man who had never loved the Emperor — a sort of monster essentially worse than a mere betrayer.

General D'Hubert shrugged his shoulders without anger at this ferocious prejudice. Rejected by his old friends, and mistrusting profoundly the advances of Royalist society, the young and handsome general (he was barely forty) adopted a manner of cold, punctilious courtesy, which at the merest shadow of an intended slight passed easily into harsh haughtiness. Thus prepared, General D'Hubert went about his affairs in Paris feeling inwardly very happy with the peculiar uplifting happiness of a man very much in love. The charming girl looked out by his sister had come upon the scene, and had conquered him in the thorough manner in which a young girl by merely existing in his sight can make a man of forty her own. They were going to be married as soon as General D'Hubert had obtained his official nomination to a promised command.

One afternoon, sitting on the terrasse of the Cafe Tortoni, General D'Hubert learned from the conversation of two strangers occupying a table near his own, that General Feraud, included in the batch of superior officers arrested after the second return of the king, was in danger of passing before the Special Commission. Living all his spare moments, as is frequently the case with expectant lovers, a day in advance of reality, and in a state of bestarred hallucination, it required nothing less than the name of his perpetual antagonist pronounced in a loud voice to call the youngest of Napoleon's generals away from the mental contemplation of his betrothed. He looked round. The strangers wore civilian clothes. Lean and weather-beaten, lolling back in their chairs, they scowled at people with moody and defiant abstraction from under their hats pulled low over their eyes. It was not difficult to recognize them for two of the compulsorily retired officers of the Old Guard. As from bravado or carelessness they chose to speak in loud tones, General D'Hubert, who saw no reason why he should change his seat, heard every word. They did not seem to be the personal friends of General Feraud. His name came up amongst others. Hearing it repeated, General D'Hubert's tender anticipations of a domestic future adorned with a woman's grace were traversed by the harsh regret of his warlike past, of that one long, intoxicating clash of arms, unique in the magnitude of its glory and disaster — the marvellous work and the special possession of his own generation. He felt an irrational tenderness towards his old adversary and appreciated emotionally the murderous absurdity their encounter had introduced into his life. It was like an additional pinch of spice in a hot dish. He remembered the flavour with sudden melancholy. He would never taste it again. It was all over. 'I fancy it was being left lying in the garden that had exasperated him so against me from the first,' he thought, indulgently.

The two strangers at the next table had fallen silent after the third mention of General Feraud's name. Presently the elder of the two, speaking again in a bitter tone, affirmed that General Feraud's account was settled. And why? Simply because he was not like some bigwigs who loved only themselves. The Royalists knew they could never make anything of him. He loved The Other too well.

The Other was the Man of St. Helena. The two officers nodded and touched glasses before they drank to an impossible return. Then the same who had spoken before, remarked with a sardonic laugh, 'His adversary showed more cleverness.'

'What adversary?' asked the younger, as if puzzled.

'Don't you know? They were two hussars. At each promotion they fought a duel. Haven't you heard of the duel going on ever since 1801?'

The other had heard of the duel, of course. Now he understood the allusion. General Baron D'Hubert would be able now to enjoy his fat king's favour in peace.

'Much good may it do to him,' mumbled the elder. 'They were both brave men. I never saw this D'Hubert — a sort of intriguing dandy, I am told. But I can well believe what I've heard Feraud say of him — that he never loved the Emperor.'

They rose and went away.

General D'Hubert experienced the horror of a somnambulist who wakes up from a complacent dream of activity to find himself walking on a quagmire. A profound disgust of the ground on which he was making his way overcame him. Even the image of the charming girl was swept from his view in the flood of moral distress. Everything he had ever been or hoped to be would taste of bitter ignominy unless he could manage to save General Feraud from the fate which threatened so many braves. Under the impulse of this almost morbid need to attend to the safety of his adversary, General D'Hubert worked so well with hands and feet (as the French saying is), that in less than twenty-four hours he found means of obtaining an extraordinary private audience from the Minister of Police.

General Baron D'Hubert was shown in suddenly without preliminaries. In the dusk of the Minister's cabinet, behind the forms of writing-desk, chairs, and tables, between two bunches of wax candles blazing in sconces, he beheld a figure in a gorgeous coat posturing before a tall mirror. The old conventionnel Fouche, Senator of the Empire, traitor to every man, to every principle and motive of human conduct. Duke of Otranto, and the wily artizan of the second Restoration, was trying the fit of a court suit in which his young and accomplished fiancee had declared her intention to have his portrait painted on porcelain. It was a caprice, a charming fancy which the first Minister of Police of the second Restoration was anxious to gratify. For that man, often compared in wiliness of conduct to a fox, but whose ethical side could be worthily symbolized by nothing less emphatic than a skunk, was as much possessed by his love as General D'Hubert himself.

Startled to be discovered thus by the

blunder of a servant, he met this little vexation with the characteristic impudence which had served his turn so well in the endless intrigues of his self-seeking career. Without altering his attitude a hair's-breadth, one leg in a silk stocking advanced, his head twisted over his left shoulder, he called out calmly, 'This way, General. Pray approach. Well? I am all attention.'

While General D'Hubert, ill at ease as if one of his own little weaknesses had been exposed, presented his request as shortly as possible, the Duke of Otranto went on feeling the fit of his collar, settling the lapels before the glass, and buckling his back in an effort to behold the set of the gold embroidered coat-skirts behind. His still face, his attentive eyes, could not have expressed a more complete interest in those matters if he had been alone.

'Exclude from the operations of the Special Court a certain Feraud, Gabriel Florian, General of brigade of the promotion of 1814?' he repeated, in a slightly wondering tone, and then turned away from the glass. 'Why exclude him precisely?'

'I am surprised that your Excellency, so competent in the evaluation of men of his time, should have thought worth while to have that name put down on the list.'

'A rabid Bonapartist!'

'So is every grenadier and every trooper of the army, as your Excellency well knows. And the individuality of General Feraud can have no more weight than that of any casual grenadier. He is a man of no mental grasp, of no capacity whatever. It is inconceivable that he should ever have any influence.'

'He has a well-hung tongue, though,' interjected Fouche.

'Noisy, I admit, but not dangerous.'

'I will not dispute with you. I know next to nothing of him. Hardly his name, in fact.'

'And yet your Excellency has the presidency of the Commission charged by the king to point out those who were to be tried,' said General D'Hubert, with an emphasis which did not miss the minister's ear.

'Yes, General,' he said, walking away into the dark part of the vast room, and throwing himself into a deep armchair that swallowed him up, all but the soft gleam of gold embroideries and the pallid patch of the face — 'yes, General. Take this chair there.'

General D'Hubert sat down.

'Yes, General,' continued the arch-master in the arts of intrigue and betrayals, whose duplicity, as if at times intolerable to his self-knowledge, found relief in bursts of cynical openness. 'I did hurry on the formation of the proscribing Commission, and I took its presidency. And do you know why? Simply from fear that if I did not take it quickly into my hands my own name would head the list of the proscribed. Such are the times in which we live. But I am minister of the king yet, and I ask you plainly why I should take the name of this obscure Feraud off the list? You wonder how his name got there! Is it possible that you should know men so little? My dear General, at the very first sitting of the Commission names poured on us like rain off the roof of the Tuileries. Names! We had our choice of thousands. How do you know that the name of this Feraud, whose life or death don't matter to France, does not keep out some other name?'

The voice out of the armchair stopped. Opposite General D'Hubert sat still, shadowy and silent. Only his sabre clinked slightly. The voice in the armchair began again. 'And we must try to satisfy the exigencies of the Allied Sovereigns, too. The Prince de Talleyrand told me only yesterday that Nesselrode had informed him officially of His Majesty the Emperor Alexander's dissatisfaction at the small number of examples the Government of the king intends to make — especially amongst military men. I tell you this confidentially.'

'Upon my word!' broke out General D'Hubert, speaking through his teeth, 'if your Excellency deigns to favour me with any more confidential information I don't know what I will do. It's enough to break one's sword over one's knee, and fling the pieces . . . '

'What government you imagined yourself to be serving?' interrupted the minister, sharply.

After a short pause the crestfallen voice of General D'Hubert answered, 'The Government of France.'

'That's paying your conscience off with mere words, General. The truth is that you are serving a government of returned exiles, of men who have been without country for twenty years. Of men also who have just got over a very bad and humiliating fright . . . Have no illusions on that score.'

The Duke of Otranto ceased. He had relieved himself, and had attained his object of stripping some self-respect off that man who had inconveniently discovered him posturing in a gold-embroidered court costume before a mirror. But they were a hot-headed lot in the army; it occurred to him that it would be inconvenient if a well-disposed general officer, received in audience on the recommendation of one of the Princes, were to do something rashly scandalous directly after a private interview with the minister. In a changed tone he put a question to the point: 'Your relation — this Feraud?'

'No. No relation at all.'

'Intimate friend?'

'Intimate . . . yes. There is between us an intimate connection of a nature which makes it a point of honour with me to try . . . '

The minister rang a bell without waiting for the end of the phrase. When the servant had gone out, after bringing in a pair of heavy silver candelabra for the writing-desk, the Duke of Otranto rose, his breast glistening all over with gold in the strong light, and taking a piece of paper out of a drawer, held it in his hand ostentatiously while he said with persuasive gentleness: 'You must not speak of breaking your sword across your knee, General. Perhaps you would never get another. The Emperor will not return this time . . . Diable d'homme! There was just a moment, here in Paris, soon after Waterloo, when he frightened me. It looked as though he were ready to begin all over again. Luckily one never does begin all over again, really. You must not think of breaking your sword, General.'

General D'Hubert, looking on the ground,

moved slightly his hand in a hopeless gesture of renunciation. The Minister of Police turned his eyes away from him, and scanned deliberately the paper he had been holding up all the time.

'There are only twenty general officers selected to be made an example of. Twenty. A round number. And let's see, Feraud . . . Ah, he's there. Gabriel Florian. Parfaitement. That's your man. Well, there will be only nineteen examples made now.'

General D'Hubert stood up feeling as though he had gone through an infectious illness. 'I must beg your Excellency to keep my interference a profound secret. I attach the greatest importance to his never learning . . . '

'Who is going to inform him, I should like to know?' said Fouche, raising his eyes curiously to General D'Hubert's tense, set face. 'Take one of these pens, and run it through the name yourself. This is the only list in existence. If you are careful to take up enough ink no one will be able to tell what was the name struck out. But, par exemple, I am not responsible for what Clarke will do with him afterwards. If he persists in being rabid he will be ordered by the Minister of War to reside in some provincial town under the supervision of the police.'

A few days later General D'Hubert was saying to his sister, after the first greetings had been got over: 'Ah, my dear Leonie! it seemed to me I couldn't get away from Paris quick enough.'

'Effect of love,' she suggested, with a malicious smile.

'And horror,' added General D'Hubert, with profound seriousness. 'I have nearly died there of . . . of nausea.'

His face was contracted with disgust. And as his sister looked at him attentively he continued, 'I have had to see Fouche. I have had an audience. I have been in his cabinet. There remains with one, who had the misfortune to breathe the air of the same room with that man, a sense of diminished dignity, an uneasy feeling of being not so clean, after all, as one hoped one was . . . But you can't understand.'

She nodded quickly several times. She understood very well, on the contrary. She knew her brother thoroughly, and liked him as he was. Moreover, the scorn and loathing of mankind were the lot of the Jacobin Fouche, who, exploiting for his own advantage every weakness, every virtue, every generous illusion of mankind, made dupes of his whole generation, and died obscurely as Duke of Otranto.

'My dear Armand,' she said, compassion-ately, 'what could you want from that man?'

'Nothing less than a life,' answered General D'Hubert. 'And I've got it. It had to be done. But I feel yet as if I could never forgive the necessity to the man I had to save.'

General Feraud, totally unable (as is the case with most of us) to comprehend what was happening to him, received the Minister of War's order to proceed at once to a small town of Central France with feelings whose natural expression consisted in a fierce rolling of the eye and savage grinding of the teeth. The passing away of the state of war, the only condition of society he had ever known, the horrible view of a world at peace, frightened him. He went away to his little town firmly convinced that this could not last. There he was informed of his retirement from the army, and that his pension (calculated on the scale of a colonel's rank) was made dependent on the correctness of his conduct, and on the good reports of the police. No longer in the army! He felt suddenly strange to the earth, like a disembodied spirit. It was impossible to exist. But at first he reacted from sheer incredulity. This could not be. He waited for thunder, earthquakes, natural cataclysms; but nothing happened. The leaden weight of an irremediable idleness descended upon General Feraud, who having no resources within himself sank into a state of awe-inspiring hebetude. He haunted the streets of the little town, gazing before him with lacklustre eyes, disregarding the hats raised on his passage; and people, nudging each other as he went by, whispered, 'That's poor General Feraud. His heart is broken. Behold how he loved the Emperor.'

The other living wreckage of Napoleonic tempest clustered round General Feraud with infinite respect. He, himself, imagined his soul to be crushed by grief. He suffered from quickly succeeding impulses to weep, to howl, to bite his fists till blood came, to spend days on his bed with his head thrust under the pillow; but these arose from sheer ennui, from the anguish of an immense, indescribable, inconceivable boredom. His mental inability to grasp the hopeless nature of his case as a whole saved him from suicide. He never even thought of it once. He thought of nothing. But his appetite abandoned him, and the difficulty he experienced to express the overwhelming nature of his feelings (the most furious swearing could do no justice to it) induced gradually a habit of silence — a sort of death to a southern temperament.

Great, therefore, was the sensation amongst the anciens militaires frequenting a certain little cafe; full of flies when one stuffy afternoon 'that poor General Feraud' let out suddenly a volley of formidable curses.

He had been sitting quietly in his own privileged corner looking through the Paris gazettes with just as much interest as a condemned man on the eve of execution could be expected to show in the news of the day. 'I'll find out presently that I am alive yet,' he declared, in a dogmatic tone. 'However, this is a private affair. An old affair of honour. Bah! Our honour does not matter. Here we are driven off with a split ear like a lot of cast troop horses — good only for a knacker's yard. But it would be like striking a blow for the Emperor ... Messieurs, I shall require the assistance of two of you.'

Every man moved forward. General Feraud, deeply touched by this demonstration, called with visible emotion upon the one-eyed veteran cuirassier and the officer of the Chasseurs a Cheval who had left the tip of his nose in Russia. He excused his choice to the others.

'A cavalry affair this — you know.'

He was answered with a varied chorus of 'Parfaitement, mon General ... C'est juste ... Parbleu, c'est connu ... ' Everybody was satisfied. The three left the cafe together, followed by cries of 'Bonne chance.'

Outside they linked arms, the general in

the middle. The three rusty cocked hats worn en bataille with a sinister forward slant barred the narrow street nearly right across. The overheated little town of grey stones and red tiles was drowsing away its provincial afternoon under a blue sky. The loud blows of a cooper hooping a cask reverberated regularly between the houses. The general dragged his left foot a little in the shade of the walls.

'This damned winter of 1813 has got into my bones for good. Never mind. We must take pistols, that's all. A little lumbago. We must have pistols. He's game for my bag. My eyes are as keen as ever. You should have seen me in Russia picking off the dodging Cossacks with a beastly old infantry musket. I have a natural gift for firearms.'

In this strain General Feraud ran on, holding up his head, with owlish eyes and rapacious beak. A mere fighter all his life, a cavalry man, a sabreur, he conceived war with the utmost simplicity, as, in the main, a massed lot of personal contests, a sort of gregarious duelling. And here he had in hand a war of his own. He revived. The shadow of peace passed away from him like the shadow of death. It was the marvellous resurrection of the named Feraud, Gabriel Florian, engage volontaire of 1793, General of 1814, buried without ceremony by means of a service order signed by the War Minister of the Second Restoration.

4

No man succeeds in everything he undertakes. In that sense we are all failures. The great point is not to fail in ordering and sustaining the effort of our life. In this matter vanity is what leads us astray. It hurries us into situations from which we must come out damaged; whereas pride is our safeguard, by the reserve it imposes on the choice of our endeavour as much as by the virtue of its sustaining power.

General D'Hubert was proud and reserved. He had not been damaged by his casual love affairs, successful or otherwise. In his war-scarred body his heart at forty remained unscratched. Entering with reserve into his sister's matrimonial plans, he had felt himself falling irremediably in love as one falls off a roof. He was too proud to be frightened. Indeed, the sensation was too delightful to be alarming.

The inexperience of a man of forty is a much more serious thing than the inexperience of a youth of twenty, for it is not helped out by the rashness of hot blood. The girl was mysterious, as young girls are by the mere effect of their guarded ingenuity; and to him the mysteriousness of that young girl appeared exceptional and fascinating. But there was nothing mysterious about the arrangements of the match which Madame Leonie had promoted. There was nothing peculiar, either. It was a very appropriate match, commending itself extremely to the young lady's mother (the father was dead) and tolerable to the young lady's uncle — an old emigre lately returned from Germany, and pervading, cane in hand, a lean ghost of the ancien regime, the garden walks of the young lady's ancestral home.

General D'Hubert was not the man to be satisfied merely with the woman and the fortune — when it came to the point. His pride (and pride aims always at true success) would be satisfied with nothing short of love. But as true pride excludes vanity, he could not imagine any reason why this mysterious creature with deep and brilliant eyes of a violet colour should have any feeling for him warmer than indifference. The young lady (her name was Adele) baffled every attempt at a clear understanding on that point. It is true that the attempts were clumsy and made timidly, because by then General D'Hubert had become acutely aware of the number of his years, of his wounds, of his many moral imperfections, of his secret unworthiness — and had incidentally learned by experience the meaning of the word funk. As far as he could make out she seemed to imply that, with an unbounded confidence in her mother's affection and sagacity, she felt no unsurmountable dislike for the person of General D'Hubert; and that this was quite sufficient for a well-brought-up young lady to begin married life upon. This view hurt and tormented the pride of General D'Hubert. And yet he asked himself, with a sort of sweet despair, what more could he expect? She had a quiet and luminous forehead. Her violet eyes laughed while the lines of her lips and chin remained composed in admirable gravity. All this was set off by such a glorious mass of fair hair, by a complexion so marvellous, by such a grace of expression, that General D'Hubert really never found the opportunity to examine with sufficient detachment the lofty exigencies of his pride. In fact, he became shy of that line of inquiry since it had led once or twice to a crisis of solitary passion in which it was borne upon him that he loved her enough to kill her rather than lose her. From such passages, not unknown to men of forty, he would come out broken, exhausted, remorseful, a little dismayed. He derived, however, considerable comfort from the quietist practice of sitting now and then half the night by an open window and meditating upon the wonder of her existence, like a believer lost in the mystic contemplation of his faith.

It must not be supposed that all these variations of his inward state were made manifest to the world. General D'Hubert found no difficulty in appearing wreathed in smiles. Because, in fact, he was very happy. He followed the established rules of his condition, sending over flowers (from his sister's garden and hot-houses) early every morning, and a little later following himself to lunch with his intended, her mother, and her emigre uncle. The middle of the day was spent in strolling or sitting in the shade. A watchful deference, trembling on the verge of tenderness was the note of their intercourse on his side — with a playful turn of the phrase concealing the profound trouble of his whole being caused by her inaccessible nearness. Late in the afternoon General D'Hubert walked home between the fields of vines, sometimes intensely miserable, sometimes supremely happy, sometimes pensively sad; but always feeling a special intensity of existence, that elation common to artists, poets, and lovers — to men haunted by a great passion, a noble thought, or a new vision of plastic beauty.

The outward world at that time did not exist with any special distinctness for General D'Hubert. One evening, however, crossing a ridge from which he could see both houses, General D'Hubert became aware of two figures far down the road. The day had been divine. The festal decoration of the inflamed sky lent a gentle glow to the sober tints of the southern land. The grey rocks, the brown fields, the purple, undulating distances harmonized in luminous accord, exhaled already the scents of the evening. The two figures down the road presented themselves like two rigid and wooden silhouettes all black on the ribbon of white dust. General D'Hubert made out the long, straight, military capotes buttoned closely right up to the black stocks, the cocked hats, the lean, carven, brown countenances — old soldiers — vieilles moustaches! The taller of the two had a black patch over one eye; the other's hard, dry countenance presented some bizarre, disquieting peculiarity, which on nearer approach proved to be the absence of the tip of the nose. Lifting their hands with one movement to salute the slightly lame civilian walking with a thick stick, they inquired for the house where the General Baron D'Hubert lived, and what was the best way to get speech with him quietly.

'If you think this quiet enough,' said General D'Hubert, looking round at the vine-fields, framed in purple lines, and dominated by the nest of grey and drab walls of a village clustering around the top of a conical hill, so that the blunt church tower seemed but the shape of a crowning rock — 'if you think this spot quiet enough, you can speak to him at once. And I beg you, comrades, to speak openly, with perfect confidence.'

They stepped back at this, and raised again their hands to their hats with marked ceremoniousness. Then the one with the chipped nose, speaking for both, remarked that the matter was confidential enough, and to be arranged discreetly. Their general quarters were established in that village over there, where the infernal clodhoppers — damn their false, Royalist hearts! — looked remarkably cross-eyed at three unassuming military men. For the present he should only ask for the name of General D'Hubert's friends.

'What friends?' said the astonished General D'Hubert, completely off the track. 'I am staying with my brother-in-law over there.'

'Well, he will do for one,' said the chipped veteran.

'We're the friends of General Feraud,'

interjected the other, who had kept silent till then, only glowering with his one eye at the man who had never loved the Emperor. That was something to look at. For even the gold-laced Judases who had sold him to the English, the marshals and princes, had loved him at some time or other. But this man had never loved the Emperor. General Feraud had said so distinctly.

General D'Hubert felt an inward blow in his chest. For an infinitesimal fraction of a second it was as if the spinning of the earth had become perceptible with an awful, slight rustle in the eternal stillness of space. But this noise of blood in his ears passed off at once. Involuntarily he murmured, 'Feraud! I had forgotten his existence.'

'He's existing at present, very uncomfortably, it is true, in the infamous inn of that nest of savages up there,' said the one-eyed cuirassier, drily. 'We arrived in your parts an hour ago on post horses. He's awaiting our return with impatience. There is hurry, you know. The General has broken the ministerial order to obtain from you the satisfaction he's entitled to by the laws of honour, and naturally he's anxious to have it all over before the gendarmerie gets on his scent.'

The other elucidated the idea a little further. 'Get back on the quiet — you understand? Phitt! No one the wiser. We have broken out, too. Your friend the king would be glad to cut off our scurvy pittances at the first chance. It's a risk. But honour before everything.'

General D'Hubert had recovered his powers of speech. 'So you come here like this along the road to invite me to a throat-cutting match with that — that . . . ' A laughing sort of rage took possession of him. 'Ha! ha! ha! ha!'

His fists on his hips, he roared without restraint, while they stood before him lank and straight, as though they had been shot up with a snap through a trap door in the ground. Only four-and-twenty months ago the masters of Europe, they had already the air of antique ghosts, they seemed less substantial in their faded coats than their own narrow shadows falling so black across the white road: the military and grotesque shadows of twenty years of war and conquests. They had an outlandish appearance of two imperturbable bonzes of the religion of the sword. And General D'Hubert, also one of the ex-masters of Europe, laughed at these serious phantoms standing in his way.

Said one, indicating the laughing General with a jerk of the head: 'A merry companion, that.'

'There are some of us that haven't smiled

from the day The Other went away,' remarked his comrade.

A violent impulse to set upon and beat those unsubstantial wraiths to the ground frightened General D'Hubert. He ceased laughing suddenly. His desire now was to get rid of them, to get them away from his sight quickly before he lost control of himself. He wondered at the fury he felt rising in his breast. But he had no time to look into that peculiarity just then.

'I understand your wish to be done with me as quickly as possible. Don't let us waste time in empty ceremonies. Do you see that wood there at the foot of that slope? Yes, the wood of pines. Let us meet there to-morrow at sunrise. I will bring with me my sword or my pistols, or both if you like.'

The seconds of General Feraud looked at each other.

'Pistols, General,' said the cuirassier.

'So be it. Au revoir — to-morrow morning. Till then let me advise you to keep close if you don't want the gendarmerie making inquiries about you before it gets dark. Strangers are rare in this part of the country.'

They saluted in silence. General D'Hubert, turning his back on their retreating forms, stood still in the middle of the road for a long time, biting his lower lip and looking on the ground. Then he began to walk straight before him, thus retracing his steps till he found himself before the park gate of his intended's house. Dusk had fallen. Motionless he stared through the bars at the front of the house, gleaming clear beyond the thickets and trees. Footsteps scrunched on the gravel, and presently a tall stooping shape emerged from the lateral alley following the inner side of the park wall.

Le Chevalier de Valmassigue, uncle of the adorable Adele, ex-brigadier in the army of the Princes, bookbinder in Altona, afterwards shoemaker (with a great reputation for elegance in the fit of ladies' shoes) in another small German town, wore silk stockings on his lean shanks, low shoes with silver buckles, a brocaded waistcoat. A long-skirted coat, a la francaise, covered loosely his thin, bowed back. A small three-cornered hat rested on a lot of powdered hair, tied in a queue.

'Monsieur le Chevalier,' called General D'Hubert, softly.

'What? You here again, mon ami? Have you forgotten something?'

'By heavens! that's just it. I have forgotten something. I am come to tell you of it. No — outside. Behind this wall. It's too ghastly a thing to be let in at all where she lives.'

The Chevalier came out at once with that

111

benevolent resignation some old people display towards the fugue of youth. Older by a quarter of a century than General D'Hubert, he looked upon him in the secret of his heart as a rather troublesome youngster in love. He had heard his enigmatical words very well, but attached no undue importance to what a mere man of forty so hard hit was likely to do or say. The turn of mind of the generation of Frenchmen grown up during the years of his exile was almost unintelligible to him. Their sentiments appeared to him unduly violent, lacking fineness and measure, their language needlessly exaggerated. He joined calmly the General on the road, and they made a few steps in silence, the General trying to master his agitation, and get proper control of his voice.

'It is perfectly true; I forgot something. I forgot till half an hour ago that I had an urgent affair of honour on my hands. It's incredible, but it is so!'

All was still for a moment. Then in the profound evening silence of the countryside the clear, aged voice of the Chevalier was heard trembling slightly: 'Monsieur! That's an indignity.'

It was his first thought. The girl born during his exile, the posthumous daughter of his poor brother murdered by a band of

Jacobins, had grown since his return very dear to his old heart, which had been starving on mere memories of affection for so many years. 'It is an inconceivable thing, I say! A man settles such affairs before he thinks of asking for a young girl's hand. Why! If you had forgotten for ten days longer, you would have been married before your memory returned to you. In my time men did not forget such things — nor yet what is due to the feelings of an innocent young woman. If I did not respect them myself, I would qualify your conduct in a way which you would not like.'

General D'Hubert relieved himself frankly by a groan. 'Don't let that consideration prevent you. You run no risk of offending her mortally.'

But the old man paid no attention to this lover's nonsense. It's doubtful whether he even heard. 'What is it?' he asked. 'What's the nature of . . . ?'

'Call it a youthful folly, Monsieur le Chevalier. An inconceivable, incredible result of . . . ' He stopped short. 'He will never believe the story,' he thought. 'He will only think I am taking him for a fool, and get offended.' General D'Hubert spoke up again: 'Yes, originating in youthful folly, it has become . . . '

The Chevalier interrupted: 'Well, then it

must be arranged.'

'Arranged?'

'Yes, no matter at what cost to your amour propre. You should have remembered you were engaged. You forgot that, too, I suppose. And then you go and forget your quarrel. It's the most hopeless exhibition of levity I ever heard of.'

'Good heavens, Monsieur! You don't imagine I have been picking up this quarrel last time I was in Paris, or anything of the sort, do you?'

'Eh! What matters the precise date of your insane conduct,' exclaimed the Chevalier, testily. 'The principal thing is to arrange it.'

Noticing General D'Hubert getting restive and trying to place a word, the old emigre raised his hand, and added with dignity, 'I've been a soldier, too. I would never dare suggest a doubtful step to the man whose name my niece is to bear. I tell you that entre galants hommes an affair can always be arranged.'

'But saperiotte, Monsieur le Chevalier, it's fifteen or sixteen years ago. I was a lieutenant of hussars then.'

The old Chevalier seemed confounded by the vehemently despairing tone of this information. 'You were a lieutenant of hussars sixteen years ago,' he mumbled in a dazed manner.

'Why, yes! You did not suppose I was made a general in my cradle like a royal prince.'

In the deepening purple twilight of the fields spread with vine leaves, backed by a low band of sombre crimson in the west, the voice of the old ex-officer in the army of the Princes sounded collected, punctiliously civil.

'Do I dream? Is this a pleasantry? Or am I to understand that you have been hatching an affair of honour for sixteen years?'

'It has clung to me for that length of time. That is my precise meaning. The quarrel itself is not to be explained easily. We met on the ground several times during that time, of course.'

'What manners! What horrible perversion of manliness! Nothing can account for such inhumanity but the sanguinary madness of the Revolution which has tainted a whole generation,' mused the returned emigre in a low tone. 'Who's your adversary?' he asked a little louder.

'My adversary? His name is Feraud.'

Shadowy in his tricorne and old-fashioned clothes, like a bowed, thin ghost of the ancien regime, the Chevalier voiced a ghostly memory. 'I can remember the feud about little Sophie Derval, between Monsieur de Brissac, Captain in the Bodyguards, and d'Anjorrant (not the pock-marked one, the other — the Beau d'Anjorrant, as they called him). They met three times in eighteen months in a most gallant manner. It was the fault of that little Sophie, too, who would keep on playing . . . '

'This is nothing of the kind,' interrupted General D'Hubert. He laughed a little sardonically. 'Not at all so simple,' he added. 'Nor yet half so reasonable,' he finished, inaudibly, between his teeth, and ground them with rage.

After this sound nothing troubled the silence for a long time, till the Chevalier asked, without animation: 'What is he — this Feraud?'

'Lieutenant of hussars, too — I mean, he's a general. A Gascon. Son of a blacksmith, I believe.'

'There! I thought so. That Bonaparte had a special predilection for the canaille. I don't mean this for you, D'Hubert. You are one of us, though you have served this usurper, who . . . '

'Let's leave him out of this,' broke in General D'Hubert.

The Chevalier shrugged his peaked shoulders. 'Feraud of sorts. Offspring of a blacksmith and some village troll. See what comes of mixing yourself up with that sort of people.'

'You have made shoes yourself, Chevalier.'

'Yes. But I am not the son of a shoemaker. Neither are you, Monsieur D'Hubert. You and I have something that your Bonaparte's princes, dukes, and marshals have not, because there's no power on earth that could give it to them,' retorted the emigre, with the rising animation of a man who has got hold of a hopeful argument. 'Those people don't exist — all these Ferauds. Feraud! What is Feraud? A va-nu-pieds disguised into a general by a Corsican adventurer masquerading as an emperor. There is no earthly reason for a D'Hubert to s'encanailler by a duel with a person of that sort. You can make your excuses to him perfectly well. And if the manant takes into his head to decline them, you may simply refuse to meet him.'

'You say I may do that?'

'I do. With the clearest conscience.'

'Monsieur le Chevalier! To what do you think you have returned from your emigration?'

This was said in such a startling tone that the old man raised sharply his bowed head, glimmering silvery white under the points of the little tricorne. For a time he made no sound.

'God knows!' he said at last, pointing with a slow and grave gesture at a tall roadside cross mounted on a block of stone, and stretching its arms of forged iron all black against the darkening red band in the sky — 'God knows! If it were not for this emblem, which I remember seeing on this spot as a child, I would wonder to what we who remained faithful to God and our king have returned. The very voices of the people have changed.'

'Yes, it is a changed France,' said General D'Hubert. He seemed to have regained his calm. His tone was slightly ironic. 'Therefore I cannot take your advice. Besides, how is one to refuse to be bitten by a dog that means to bite? It's impracticable. Take my word for it — Feraud isn't a man to be stayed by apologies or refusals. But there are other ways. I could, for instance, send a messenger with a word to the brigadier of the gendarmerie in Senlac. He and his two friends are liable to arrest on my simple order. It would make some talk in the army, both the organized and the disbanded — especially the disbanded. All canaille! All once upon a time the companions in arms of Armand D'Hubert. But what need a D'Hubert care what people that don't exist may think? Or, better still, I might get my brother-in-law to send for the mayor of the village and give him a hint. No more would be needed to get the three 'brigands' set upon with flails and pitchforks and hunted into some nice, deep, wet ditch — and nobody the wiser! It has been done only ten miles from here to three poor devils of the disbanded Red Lancers of the Guard going to their homes. What says your conscience, Chevalier? Can a D'Hubert do that thing to three men who do not exist?'

A few stars had come out on the blue obscurity, clear as crystal, of the sky. The dry, thin voice of the Chevalier spoke harshly: 'Why are you telling me all this?'

The General seized the withered old hand with a strong grip. 'Because I owe you my fullest confidence. Who could tell Adele but you? You understand why I dare not trust my brother-in-law nor yet my own sister. Chevalier! I have been so near doing these things that I tremble yet. You don't know how terrible this duel appears to me. And there's no escape from it.'

He murmured after a pause, 'It's a fatality,' dropped the Chevalier's passive hand, and said in his ordinary conversational voice, 'I shall have to go without seconds. If it is my lot to remain on the ground, you at least will know all that can be made known of this affair.'

The shadowy ghost of the ancien regime

seemed to have become more bowed during the conversation. 'How am I to keep an indifferent face this evening before these two women?' he groaned. 'General! I find it very difficult to forgive you.'

General D'Hubert made no answer.

'Is your cause good, at least?'

'I am innocent.'

This time he seized the Chevalier's ghostly arm above the elbow, and gave it a mighty squeeze. 'I must kill him!' he hissed, and opening his hand strode away down the road.

The delicate attentions of his adoring sister had secured for the General perfect liberty of movement in the house where he was a guest. He had even his own entrance through a small door in one corner of the orangery. Thus he was not exposed that evening to the necessity of dissembling his agitation before the calm ignorance of the other inmates. He was glad of it. It seemed to him that if he had to open his lips he would break out into horrible and aimless imprecations, start breaking furniture, smashing china and glass. From the moment he opened the private door and while ascending the twenty-eight steps of a winding staircase, giving access to the corridor on which his room opened, he went through a horrible and humiliating scene in which an infuriated madman with blood-shot eyes and a foaming mouth played inconceivable havoc with everything inanimate that may be found in a well-appointed dining-room. When he opened the door of his apartment the fit was over, and his bodily fatigue was so great that he had to catch at the backs of the chairs while crossing the room to reach a low and broad divan on which he let himself fall heavily. His moral prostration was still greater. That brutality of feeling which he had known only when charging the enemy, sabre in hand, amazed this man of forty, who did not recognize in it the instinctive fury of his menaced passion. But in his mental and bodily exhaustion this passion got cleared, distilled, refined into a sentiment of melancholy despair at having, perhaps, to die before he had taught this beautiful girl to love him.

That night, General D'Hubert stretched out on his back with his hands over his eyes, or lying on his breast with his face buried in a cushion, made the full pilgrimage of emotions. Nauseating disgust at the absurdity of the situation, doubt of his own fitness to conduct his existence, and mistrust of his best sentiments (for what the devil did he want to go to Fouche for?) — he knew them all in turn. 'I am an idiot, neither more nor less,' he thought — 'A sensitive idiot. Because I overheard two men talking in a cafe . . . I am an idiot afraid of lies — whereas in life it is only truth that matters.'

Several times he got up and, walking in his socks in order not to be heard by anybody downstairs, drank all the water he could find in the dark. And he tasted the torments of jealousy, too. She would marry somebody else. His very soul writhed. The tenacity of that Feraud, the awful persistence of that imbecile brute, came to him with the tremendous force of a relentless destiny. General D'Hubert trembled as he put down the empty water ewer. 'He will have me,' he thought. General D'Hubert was tasting every emotion that life has to give. He had in his dry mouth the faint sickly flavour of fear, not the excusable fear before a young girl's candid and amused glance, but the fear of death and the honourable man's fear of cowardice.

But if true courage consists in going out to meet an odious danger from which our body, soul, and heart recoil together, General D'Hubert had the opportunity to practise it for the first time in his life. He had charged exultingly at batteries and at infantry squares, and ridden with messages through a hail of bullets without thinking anything about it. His business now was to sneak out unheard, at break of day, to an obscure and revolting death. General D'Hubert never hesitated. He carried two pistols in a leather bag which he slung over his shoulder. Before he had crossed the garden his mouth was dry again. He picked two oranges. It was only after shutting the gate after him that he felt a slight faintness.

He staggered on, disregarding it, and after going a few yards regained the command of his legs. In the colourless and pellucid dawn the wood of pines detached its columns of trunks and its dark green canopy very clearly against the rocks of the grey hillside. He kept his eyes fixed on it steadily, and sucked at an orange as he walked. That temperamental good-humoured coolness in the face of danger which had made him an officer liked by his men and appreciated by his superiors was gradually asserting itself. It was like going into battle. Arriving at the edge of the wood he sat down on a boulder, holding the other orange in his hand, and reproached himself for coming so ridiculously early on the ground. Before very long, however, he heard the swishing of bushes, footsteps on the hard ground, and the sounds of a disjointed, loud conversation. A voice somewhere behind him said boastfully, 'He's game for my bag.'

He thought to himself, 'Here they are.

What's this about game? Are they talking of me?' And becoming aware of the other orange in his hand, he thought further, 'These are very good oranges. Leonie's own tree. I may just as well eat this orange now instead of flinging it away.'

Emerging from a wilderness of rocks and bushes, General Feraud and his seconds discovered General D'Hubert engaged in peeling the orange. They stood still, waiting till he looked up. Then the seconds raised their hats, while General Feraud, putting his hands behind his back, walked aside a little way.

'I am compelled to ask one of you, messieurs, to act for me. I have brought no friends. Will you?'

The one-eyed cuirassier said judicially, 'That cannot be refused.'

The other veteran remarked, 'It's awkward all the same.'

'Owing to the state of the people's minds in this part of the country there was no one I could trust safely with the object of your presence here,' explained General D'Hubert, urbanely.

They saluted, looked round, and remarked both together:

'Poor ground.'

'It's unfit.'

'Why bother about ground, measurements,

and so on? Let us simplify matters. Load the two pairs of pistols. I will take those of General Feraud, and let him take mine. Or, better still, let us take a mixed pair. One of each pair. Then let us go into the wood and shoot at sight, while you remain outside. We did not come here for ceremonies, but for war — war to the death. Any ground is good enough for that. If I fall, you must leave me where I lie and clear out. It wouldn't be healthy for you to be found hanging about here after that.'

It appeared after a short parley that General Feraud was willing to accept these conditions. While the seconds were loading the pistols, he could be heard whistling, and was seen to rub his hands with perfect contentment. He flung off his coat briskly, and General D'Hubert took off his own and folded it carefully on a stone.

'Suppose you take your principal to the other side of the wood and let him enter exactly in ten minutes from now,' suggested General D'Hubert, calmly, but feeling as if he were giving directions for his own execution. This, however, was his last moment of weakness. 'Wait. Let us compare watches first.'

He pulled out his own. The officer with the chipped nose went over to borrow the watch of General Feraud. They bent their heads over them for a time.

'That's it. At four minutes to six by yours. Seven to by mine.'

It was the cuirassier who remained by the side of General D'Hubert, keeping his one eye fixed immovably on the white face of the watch he held in the palm of his hand. He opened his mouth, waiting for the beat of the last second long before he snapped out the word, 'Avancez.'

General D'Hubert moved on, passing from the glaring sunshine of the Provencal morning into the cool and aromatic shade of the pines. The ground was clear between the reddish trunks, whose multitude, leaning at slightly different angles, confused his eye at first. It was like going into battle. The commanding quality of confidence in himself woke up in his breast. He was all to his affair. The problem was how to kill the adversary. Nothing short of that would free him from this imbecile nightmare. 'It's no use wounding that brute,' thought General D'Hubert. He was known as a resourceful officer. His comrades years ago used also to call him The Strategist. And it was a fact that he could think in the presence of the enemy. Whereas Feraud had been always a mere fighter — but a dead shot, unluckily.

'I must draw his fire at the greatest possible

range,' said General D'Hubert to himself.

At that moment he saw something white moving far off between the trees — the shirt of his adversary. He stepped out at once between the trunks, exposing himself freely; then, quick as lightning, leaped back. It had been a risky move but it succeeded in its object. Almost simultaneously with the pop of a shot a small piece of bark chipped off by the bullet stung his ear painfully.

General Feraud, with one shot expended, was getting cautious. Peeping round the tree, General D'Hubert could not see him at all. This ignorance of the foe's whereabouts carried with it a sense of insecurity. General D'Hubert felt himself abominably exposed on his flank and rear. Again something white fluttered in his sight. Ha! The enemy was still on his front, then. He had feared a turning movement. But apparently General Feraud was not thinking of it. General D'Hubert saw him pass without special haste from one tree to another in the straight line of approach. With great firmness of mind General D'Hubert stayed his hand. Too far yet. He knew he was no marksman. His must be a waiting game — to kill.

Wishing to take advantage of the greater thickness of the trunk, he sank down to the ground. Extended at full length, head on to his enemy, he had his person completely protected. Exposing himself would not do now, because the other was too near by this time. A conviction that Feraud would presently do something rash was like balm to General D'Hubert's soul. But to keep his chin raised off the ground was irksome, and not much use either. He peeped round, exposing a fraction of his head with dread, but really with little risk. His enemy, as a matter of fact, did not expect to see anything of him so far down as that. General D'Hubert caught a fleeting view of General Feraud shifting trees again with deliberate caution. 'He despises my shooting,' he thought, displaying that insight into the mind of his antagonist which is of such great help in winning battles. He was confirmed in his tactics of immobility. 'If I could only watch my rear as well as my front!' he thought anxiously, longing for the impossible.

It required some force of character to lay his pistols down; but, on a sudden impulse, General D'Hubert did this very gently — one on each side of him. In the army he had been looked upon as a bit of a dandy because he used to shave and put on a clean shirt on the days of battle. As a matter of fact, he had always been very careful of his personal appearance. In a man of nearly forty, in love with a young and charming girl, this praiseworthy self-respect may run to such little weaknesses as, for instance, being provided with an elegant little leather folding-case containing a small ivory comb, and fitted with a piece of looking-glass on the outside. General D'Hubert, his hands being free, felt in his breeches' pockets for that implement of innocent vanity excusable in the possessor of long, silky moustaches. He drew it out, and then with the utmost coolness and promptitude turned himself over on his back. In this new attitude, his head a little raised, holding the little looking-glass just clear of his tree, he squinted into it with his left eye, while the right kept a direct watch on the rear of his position. Thus was proved Napoleon's saying, that 'for a French soldier, the word impossible does not exist.' He had the right tree nearly filling the field of his little mirror.

'If he moves from behind it,' he reflected with satisfaction, 'I am bound to see his legs. But in any case he can't come upon me unawares.'

And sure enough he saw the boots of General Feraud flash in and out, eclipsing for an instant everything else reflected in the little mirror. He shifted its position accordingly. But having to form his judgment of the change from that indirect view he did not realize that now his feet and a portion of his legs were in plain sight of General Feraud.

General Feraud had been getting gradually impressed by the amazing cleverness with which his enemy was keeping cover. He had spotted the right tree with bloodthirsty precision. He was absolutely certain of it. And yet he had not been able to glimpse as much as the tip of an ear. As he had been looking for it at the height of about five feet ten inches from the ground it was no great wonder — but it seemed very wonderful to General Feraud.

The first view of these feet and legs determined a rush of blood to his head. He literally staggered behind his tree, and had to steady himself against it with his hand. The other was lying on the ground, then! On the ground! Perfectly still, too! Exposed! What could it mean? . . . The notion that he had knocked over his adversary at the first shot entered then General Feraud's head. Once there it grew with every second of attentive gazing, overshadowing every other supposition — irresistible, triumphant, ferocious.

'What an ass I was to think I could have missed him,' he muttered to himself. 'He was exposed en plein — the fool! — for quite a couple of seconds.'

General Feraud gazed at the motionless

limbs, the last vestiges of surprise fading before an unbounded admiration of his own deadly skill with the pistol.

'Turned up his toes! By the god of war, that was a shot!' he exulted mentally. 'Got it through the head, no doubt, just where I aimed, staggered behind that tree, rolled over on his back, and died.'

And he stared! He stared, forgetting to move, almost awed, almost sorry. But for nothing in the world would he have had it undone. Such a shot! — such a shot! Rolled over on his back and died!

For it was this helpless position, lying on the back, that shouted its direct evidence at General Feraud! It never occurred to him that it might have been deliberately assumed by a living man. It was inconceivable. It was beyond the range of sane supposition. There was no possibility to guess the reason for it. And it must be said, too, that General D'Hubert's turned-up feet looked thoroughly dead. General Feraud expanded his lungs for a stentorian shout to his seconds, but, from what he felt to be an excessive scrupulousness, refrained for a while.

'I will just go and see first whether he breathes yet,' he mumbled to himself, leaving carelessly the shelter of his tree. This move was immediately perceived by the resourceful

General D'Hubert. He concluded it to be another shift, but when he lost the boots out of the field of the mirror he became uneasy. General Feraud had only stepped a little out of the line, but his adversary could not possibly have supposed him walking up with perfect unconcern. General D'Hubert, beginning to wonder at what had become of the other, was taken unawares so completely that the first warning of danger consisted in the long, early-morning shadow of his enemy falling aslant on his outstretched legs. He had not even heard a footfall on the soft ground between the trees!

It was too much even for his coolness. He jumped up thoughtlessly, leaving the pistols on the ground. The irresistible instinct of an average man (unless totally paralyzed by discomfiture) would have been to stoop for his weapons, exposing himself to the risk of being shot down in that position. Instinct, of course, is irreflective. It is its very definition. But it may be an inquiry worth pursuing whether in reflective mankind the mechanical promptings of instinct are not affected by the customary mode of thought. In his young days, Armand D'Hubert, the reflective, promising officer, had emitted the opinion that in warfare one should 'never cast back on the lines of a mistake.' This idea, defended and developed in many discussions, had settled into one of the stock notions of his brain, had become a part of his mental individuality. Whether it had gone so inconceivably deep as to affect the dictates of his instinct, or simply because, as he himself declared afterwards, he was 'too scared to remember the confounded pistols,' the fact is that General D'Hubert never attempted to stoop for them. Instead of going back on his mistake, he seized the rough trunk with both hands, and swung himself behind it with such impetuosity that, going right round in the very flash and report of the pistol-shot, he reappeared on the other side of the tree face to face with General Feraud. This last, completely unstrung by such a show of agility on the part of a dead man, was trembling yet. A very faint mist of smoke hung before his face which had an extraordinary aspect, as if the lower jaw had come unhinged.

'Not missed!' he croaked, hoarsely, from the depths of a dry throat.

This sinister sound loosened the spell that had fallen on General D'Hubert's senses. 'Yes, missed — a bout portant,' he heard himself saying, almost before he had recovered the full command of his faculties. The revulsion of feeling was accompanied by a gust of homicidal fury, resuming in its violence the accumulated resentment of a lifetime. For years General D'Hubert had been exasperated and humiliated by an atrocious absurdity imposed upon him by this man's savage caprice. Besides, General D'Hubert had been in this last instance too unwilling to confront death for the reaction of his anguish not to take the shape of a desire to kill. 'And I have my two shots to fire yet,' he added, pitilessly.

General Feraud snapped-to his teeth, and his face assumed an irate, undaunted expression. 'Go on!' he said, grimly.

These would have been his last words if General D'Hubert had been holding the pistols in his hands. But the pistols were lying on the ground at the foot of a pine. General D'Hubert had the second of leisure necessary to remember that he had dreaded death not as a man, but as a lover; not as a danger, but as a rival; not as a foe to life, but as an obstacle to marriage. And behold! there was the rival defeated! — utterly defeated, crushed, done for!

He picked up the weapons mechanically, and, instead of firing them into General Feraud's breast, he gave expression to the thoughts uppermost in his mind, 'You will fight no more duels now.'

His tone of leisurely, ineffable satisfaction

was too much for General Feraud's stoicism. 'Don't dawdle, then, damn you for a cold-blooded staff-coxcomb!' he roared out, suddenly, out of an impassive face held erect on a rigidly still body.

General D'Hubert uncocked the pistols carefully. This proceeding was observed with mixed feelings by the other general. 'You missed me twice,' the victor said, coolly, shifting both pistols to one hand; 'the last time within a foot or so. By every rule of single combat your life belongs to me. That does not mean that I want to take it now.'

'I have no use for your forbearance,' muttered General Feraud, gloomily.

'Allow me to point out that this is no concern of mine,' said General D'Hubert, whose every word was dictated by a consummate delicacy of feeling. In anger he could have killed that man, but in cold blood he recoiled from humiliating by a show of generosity this unreasonable being — a fellow-soldier of the Grande Armee, a companion in the wonders and terrors of the great military epic. 'You don't set up the pretension of dictating to me what I am to do with what's my own.'

General Feraud looked startled, and the other continued, 'You've forced me on a point of honour to keep my life at your disposal, as it were, for fifteen years. Very well. Now that the matter is decided to my advantage, I am going to do what I like with your life on the same principle. You shall keep it at my disposal as long as I choose. Neither more nor less. You are on your honour till I say the word.'

'I am! But, sacrebleu! This is an absurd position for a General of the Empire to be placed in!' cried General Feraud, in accents of profound and dismayed conviction. 'It amounts to sitting all the rest of my life with a loaded pistol in a drawer waiting for your word. It's — it's idiotic; I shall be an object of — of — derision.'

'Absurd? — idiotic? Do you think so?' queried General D'Hubert with sly gravity. 'Perhaps. But I don't see how that can be helped. However, I am not likely to talk at large of this adventure. Nobody need ever know anything about it. Just as no one to this day, I believe, knows the origin of our quarrel . . . Not a word more,' he added, hastily. 'I can't really discuss this question with a man who, as far as I am concerned, does not exist.'

When the two duellists came out into the open, General Feraud walking a little behind, and rather with the air of walking in a trance, the two seconds hurried towards them, each from his station at the edge of the wood.

General D'Hubert addressed them, speaking loud and distinctly, 'Messieurs, I make it a point of declaring to you solemnly, in the presence of General Feraud, that our difference is at last settled for good. You may inform all the world of that fact.'

'A reconciliation, after all!' they exclaimed together.

'Reconciliation? Not that exactly. It is something much more binding. Is it not so, General?'

General Feraud only lowered his head in sign of assent. The two veterans looked at each other. Later in the day, when they found themselves alone out of their moody friend's earshot, the cuirassier remarked suddenly, 'Generally speaking, I can see with my one eye as far as most people; but this beats me. He won't say anything.'

'In this affair of honour I understand there has been from first to last always something that no one in the army could quite make out,' declared the chasseur with the imperfect nose. 'In mystery it began, in mystery it went on, in mystery it is to end, apparently.'

General D'Hubert walked home with long, hasty strides, by no means uplifted by a sense of triumph. He had conquered, yet it did not seem to him that he had gained very much by his conquest. The night before he had grudged the risk of his life which appeared to him magnificent, worthy of preservation as an opportunity to win a girl's love. He had known moments when, by a marvellous illusion, this love seemed to be already his, and his threatened life a still more magnificent opportunity of devotion. Now that his life was safe it had suddenly lost its special magnificence. It had acquired instead a specially alarming aspect as a snare for the exposure of unworthiness. As to the marvellous illusion of conquered love that had visited him for a moment in the agitated watches of the night, which might have been his last on earth, he comprehended now its true nature. It had been merely a paroxysm of delirious conceit. Thus to this man, sobered by the victorious issue of a duel, life appeared robbed of its charm, simply because it was no longer menaced.

Approaching the house from the back, through the orchard and the kitchen garden, he could not notice the agitation which reigned in front. He never met a single soul. Only while walking softly along the corridor, he became aware that the house was awake and more noisy than usual. Names of servants were being called out down below in a confused noise of coming and going. With some concern he noticed that the door of his own room stood ajar, though the shutters had not been opened yet. He had hoped that his early excursion would have passed unperceived. He expected to find some servant just gone in; but the sunshine filtering through the usual cracks enabled him to see lying on the low divan something bulky, which had the appearance of two women clasped in each other's arms. Tearful and desolate murmurs issued mysteriously from that appearance. General D'Hubert pulled open the nearest pair of shutters violently. One of the women then jumped up. It was his sister. She stood for a moment with her hair hanging down and her arms raised straight up above her head, and then flung herself with a stifled cry into his arms. He returned her embrace, trying at the same time to disengage himself from it. The other woman had not risen. She seemed, on the contrary, to cling closer to the divan, hiding her face in the cushions. Her hair was also loose; it was admirably fair. General D'Hubert recognized it with staggering emotion. Mademoiselle de Valmassigue! Adele! In distress!

He became greatly alarmed, and got rid of his sister's hug definitely. Madame Leonie then extended her shapely bare arm out of her peignoir, pointing dramatically at the divan. 'This poor, terrified child has rushed here from home, on foot, two miles — running all the way.'

'What on earth has happened?' asked General D'Hubert in a low, agitated voice.

But Madame Leonie was speaking loudly. 'She rang the great bell at the gate and roused all the household — we were all asleep yet. You may imagine what a terrible shock . . . Adele, my dear child, sit up.'

General D'Hubert's expression was not that of a man who 'imagines' with facility. He did, however, fish out of the chaos of surmises the notion that his prospective mother-in-law had died suddenly, but only to dismiss it at once. He could not conceive the nature of the event or the catastrophe which would induce Mademoiselle de Valmassigue, living in a house full of servants, to bring the news over the fields herself, two miles, running all the way.

'But why are you in this room?' he whispered, full of awe.

'Of course, I ran up to see, and this child . . . I did not notice it . . . she followed me. It's that absurd Chevalier,' went on Madame Leonie, looking towards the divan . . . 'Her hair is all come down. You may imagine she did not stop to call her maid to dress it before she started . . . Adele, my dear, sit up . . . He blurted it all out to her at half-past five in the

140

morning. She woke up early and opened her shutters to breathe the fresh air, and saw him sitting collapsed on a garden bench at the end of the great alley. At that hour — you may imagine! And the evening before he had declared himself indisposed. She hurried on some clothes and flew down to him. One would be anxious for less. He loves her, but not very intelligently. He had been up all night, fully dressed, the poor old man, perfectly exhausted. He wasn't in a state to invent a plausible story . . . What a confidant you chose there! My husband was furious. He said, 'We can't interfere now.' So we sat down to wait. It was awful. And this poor child running with her hair loose over here publicly! She has been seen by some people in the fields. She has roused the whole household, too. It's awkward for her. Luckily you are to be married next week . . . Adele, sit up. He has come home on his own legs . . . We expected to see you coming on a stretcher, perhaps — what do I know? Go and see if the carriage is ready. I must take this child home at once. It isn't proper for her to stay here a minute longer.'

General D'Hubert did not move. It was as though he had heard nothing. Madame Leonie changed her mind. 'I will go and see myself,' she cried. 'I want also my cloak.

— Adele — ' she began, but did not add 'sit up.' She went out saying, in a very loud and cheerful tone: 'I leave the door open.'

General D'Hubert made a movement towards the divan, but then Adele sat up, and that checked him dead. He thought, 'I haven't washed this morning. I must look like an old tramp. There's earth on the back of my coat and pine-needles in my hair.' It occurred to him that the situation required a good deal of circumspection on his part.

'I am greatly concerned, mademoiselle,' he began, vaguely, and abandoned that line. She was sitting up on the divan with her cheeks unusually pink and her hair, brilliantly fair, falling all over her shoulders — which was a very novel sight to the general. He walked away up the room, and looking out of the window for safety said, 'I fear you must think I behaved like a madman,' in accents of sincere despair. Then he spun round, and noticed that she had followed him with her eyes. They were not cast down on meeting his glance. And the expression of her face was novel to him also. It was, one might have said, reversed. Those eyes looked at him with grave thoughtfulness, while the exquisite lines of her mouth seemed to suggest a restrained smile. This change made her transcendental beauty much less mysterious, much more

142

accessible to a man's comprehension. An amazing ease of mind came to the general — and even some ease of manner. He walked down the room with as much pleasurable excitement as he would have found in walking up to a battery vomiting death, fire, and smoke; then stood looking down with smiling eyes at the girl whose marriage with him (next week) had been so carefully arranged by the wise, the good, the admirable Leonie.

'Ah! mademoiselle,' he said, in a tone of courtly regret, 'if only I could be certain that you did not come here this morning, two miles, running all the way, merely from affection for your mother!'

He waited for an answer imperturbable but inwardly elated. It came in a demure murmur, eyelashes lowered with fascinating effect. 'You must not be mechant as well as mad.'

And then General D'Hubert made an aggressive movement towards the divan which nothing could check. That piece of furniture was not exactly in the line of the open door. But Madame Leonie, coming back wrapped up in a light cloak and carrying a lace shawl on her arm for Adele to hide her incriminating hair under, had a swift impression of her brother getting up from his knees.

'Come along, my dear child,' she cried from the doorway.

The general, now himself again in the fullest sense, showed the readiness of a resourceful cavalry officer and the peremptoriness of a leader of men. 'You don't expect her to walk to the carriage,' he said, indignantly. 'She isn't fit. I shall carry her downstairs.'

This he did slowly, followed by his awed and respectful sister; but he rushed back like a whirlwind to wash off all the signs of the night of anguish and the morning of war, and to put on the festive garments of a conqueror before hurrying over to the other house. Had it not been for that, General D'Hubert felt capable of mounting a horse and pursuing his late adversary in order simply to embrace him from excess of happiness. 'I owe it all to this stupid brute,' he thought. 'He has made plain in a morning what might have taken me years to find out — for I am a timid fool. No self-confidence whatever. Perfect coward. And the Chevalier! Delightful old man!' General D'Hubert longed to embrace him also.

The Chevalier was in bed. For several days he was very unwell. The men of the Empire and the post-revolution young ladies were too much for him. He got up the day before the wedding, and, being curious by nature, took his niece aside for a quiet talk. He advised her to find out from her husband the true story of the affair of honour, whose claim, so imperative and so persistent, had led her to within an ace of tragedy. 'It is right that his wife should be told. And next month or so will be your time to learn from him anything you want to know, my dear child.'

Later on, when the married couple came on a visit to the mother of the bride, Madame la Generale D'Hubert communicated to her beloved old uncle the true story she had obtained without any difficulty from her husband.

The Chevalier listened with deep attention to the end, took a pinch of snuff, flicked the grains of tobacco from the frilled front of his shirt, and asked, calmly, 'And that's all it was?'

'Yes, uncle,' replied Madame la Generale, opening her pretty eyes very wide. 'Isn't it funny? C'est insense — to think what men are capable of!'

'H'm!' commented the old emigre. 'It depends what sort of men. That Bonaparte's soldiers were savages. It is insense. As a wife, my dear, you must believe implicitly what your husband says.'

But to Leonie's husband the Chevalier confided his true opinion. 'If that's the tale the fellow made up for his wife, and during the honeymoon, too, you may depend on it that no one will ever know now the secret of this affair.'

Considerably later still, General D'Hubert judged the time come, and the opportunity propitious to write a letter to General Feraud. This letter began by disclaiming all animosity. 'I've never,' wrote the General Baron D'Hubert, 'wished for your death during all the time of our deplorable quarrel. Allow me,' he continued, 'to give you back in all form your forfeited life. It is proper that we two, who have been partners in so much military glory, should be friendly to each other publicly.'

The same letter contained also an item of domestic information. It was in reference to this last that General Feraud answered from a little village on the banks of the Garonne, in the following words:

'If one of your boy's names had been Napoleon — or Joseph — or even Joachim, I could congratulate you on the event with a better heart. As you have thought proper to give him the names of Charles Henri Armand, I am confirmed in my conviction that you never loved the Emperor. The thought of that sublime hero chained to a rock in the middle of a savage ocean makes life of so little value that I would receive with positive joy your instructions to blow my brains out. From suicide I consider myself in honour debarred. But I keep a loaded pistol in my drawer.'

Madame la Generale D'Hubert lifted up her hands in despair after perusing that answer.

'You see? He won't be reconciled,' said her husband. 'He must never, by any chance, be allowed to guess where the money comes from. It wouldn't do. He couldn't bear it.'

'You are a brave homme, Armand,' said Madame la Generale, appreciatively.

'My dear, I had the right to blow his brains out; but as I didn't, we can't let him starve. He has lost his pension and he is utterly incapable of doing anything in the world for himself. We must take care of him, secretly, to the end of his days. Don't I owe him the most ecstatic moment of my life? . . . Ha! ha! ha! Over the fields, two miles, running all the way! I couldn't believe my ears! . . . But for his stupid ferocity, it would have taken me years to find you out. It's extraordinary how in one way or another this man has managed to fasten himself on my deeper feelings.'

COLONEL CHABERT

To Madame la Comtesse Ida de Bocarme
nee du Chasteler

1

'Hullo! There is that old Box-coat again!'

This exclamation was made by a lawyer's clerk of the class called in French offices a gutter-jumper — a messenger in fact — who at this moment was eating a piece of dry bread with a hearty appetite. He pulled off a morsel of crumb to make into a bullet, and fired it gleefully through the open pane of the window against which he was leaning. The pellet, well aimed, rebounded almost as high as the window, after hitting the hat of a stranger who was crossing the courtyard of a house in the Rue Vivienne, where dwelt Maitre Derville, attorney-at-law.

'Come, Simonnin, don't play tricks on people, or I will turn you out of doors. However poor a client may be, he is still a man, hang it all!' said the head clerk, pausing in the addition of a bill of costs.

The lawyer's messenger is commonly, as was Simonnin, a lad of thirteen or fourteen, who, in every office, is under the special jurisdiction of the managing clerk, whose errands and *billets-doux* keep him employed on his way to carry writs to the bailiffs and petitions to the Courts. He is akin to the street boy in his habits, and to the pettifogger by fate. The boy is almost always ruthless, unbroken, unmanageable, a ribald rhymester, impudent, greedy, and idle. And yet, almost all these clerklings have an old mother lodging on some fifth floor with whom they share their pittance of thirty or forty francs a month.

'If he is a man, why do you call him old Box-coat?' asked Simonnin, with the air of a schoolboy who has caught out his master.

And he went on eating his bread and cheese, leaning his shoulder against the window jamb; for he rested standing like a cab-horse, one of his legs raised and propped against the other, on the toe of his shoe.

'What trick can we play that cove?' said the third clerk, whose name was Godeschal, in a low voice, pausing in the middle of a discourse he was extemporizing in an appeal engrossed by the fourth clerk, of which copies were being made by two neophytes from the provinces.

Then he went on improvising:

'*But, in his noble and beneficent wisdom, his Majesty, Louis the Eighteenth* — (write it at full length, heh! Desroches the learned — you, as you engross it!) — *when he resumed the reins of Government, understood* — (what

154

did that old nincompoop ever understand?) — *the high mission to which he had been called by Divine Providence!* — (a note of admiration and six stops. They are pious enough at the Courts to let us put six) — *and his first thought, as is proved by the date of the order hereinafter designated, was to repair the misfortunes caused by the terrible and sad disasters of the revolutionary times, by restoring to his numerous and faithful adherents* — ('numerous' is flattering, and ought to please the Bench) — *all their unsold estates, whether within our realm, or in conquered or acquired territory, or in the endowments of public institutions, for we are, and proclaim ourselves competent to declare, that this is the spirit and meaning of the famous, truly loyal order given in* — Stop,' said Godeschal to the three copying clerks, 'that rascally sentence brings me to the end of my page. — Well,' he went on, wetting the back fold of the sheet with his tongue, so as to be able to fold back the page of thick stamped paper, 'well, if you want to play him a trick, tell him that the master can only see his clients between two and three in the morning; we shall see if he comes, the old ruffian!'

And Godeschal took up the sentence he was dictating — '*given in* — Are you ready?'

'Yes,' cried the three writers.

It all went all together, the appeal, the gossip, and the conspiracy.

'*Given in* — Here, Daddy Boucard, what is the date of the order? We must dot our *i*'s and cross our *t*'s, by Jingo! it helps to fill the pages.'

'By Jingo!' repeated one of the copying clerks before Boucard, the head clerk, could reply.

'What! have you written *by Jingo*?' cried Godeschal, looking at one of the novices, with an expression at once stern and humorous.

'Why, yes,' said Desroches, the fourth clerk, leaning across his neighbor's copy, 'he has written, '*We must dot our i*'s' and spelt it *by Gingo!*'

All the clerks shouted with laughter.

'Why! Monsieur Hure, you take 'By Jingo' for a law term, and you say you come from Mortagne!' exclaimed Simonnin.

'Scratch it cleanly out,' said the head clerk. 'If the judge, whose business it is to tax the bill, were to see such things, he would say you were laughing at the whole boiling. You would hear of it from the chief! Come, no more of this nonsense, Monsieur Hure! A Norman ought not to write out an appeal without thought. It is the 'Shoulder arms!' of the law.'

'*Given in* — *in?*' asked Godeschal. — 'Tell me when, Boucard.'

'June 1814,' replied the head clerk, without looking up from his work.

A knock at the office door interrupted the circumlocutions of the prolix document. Five clerks with rows of hungry teeth, bright, mocking eyes, and curly heads, lifted their noses towards the door, after crying all together in a singing tone, 'Come in!'

Boucard kept his face buried in a pile of papers — *broutilles* (odds and ends) in French law jargon — and went on drawing out the bill of costs on which he was busy.

The office was a large room furnished with the traditional stool which is to be seen in all these dens of law-quibbling. The stove-pipe crossed the room diagonally to the chimney of a bricked-up fireplace; on the marble chimney-piece were several chunks of bread, triangles of Brie cheese, pork cutlets, glasses, bottles, and the head clerk's cup of chocolate. The smell of these dainties blended so completely with that of the immoderately overheated stove and the odour peculiar to offices and old papers, that the trail of a fox would not have been perceptible. The floor was covered with mud and snow, brought in by the clerks. Near the window stood the desk with a revolving lid, where the head clerk worked, and against the back of it was the second clerk's table. The second clerk was at this moment in Court. It was between eight and nine in the morning.

The only decoration of the office consisted in huge yellow posters, announcing seizures of real estate, sales, settlements under trust, final or interim judgments, — all the glory of a lawyer's office. Behind the head clerk was an enormous room, of which each division was crammed with bundles of papers with an infinite number of tickets hanging from them at the ends of red tape, which give a peculiar physiognomy to law papers. The lower rows were filled with cardboard boxes, yellow with use, on which might be read the names of the more important clients whose cases were juicily stewing at this present time. The dirty window-panes admitted but little daylight. Indeed, there are very few offices in Paris where it is possible to write without lamplight before ten in the morning in the month of February, for they are all left to very natural neglect; every one comes and no one stays; no one has any personal interest in a scene of mere routine — neither the attorney, nor the counsel, nor the clerks, trouble themselves about the appearance of a place which, to the youths, is a schoolroom; to the clients, a passage; to the chief, a laboratory. The greasy furniture is handed down to successive owners with such scrupulous care, that in some offices may still be seen boxes of *remainders*, machines for twisting parchment gut, and bags left by the prosecuting parties of the Chatelet (abbreviated to *Chlet*) — a Court which, under the old order of things, represented the present Court of First Instance (or County Court).

So in this dark office, thick with dust, there was, as in all its fellows, something repulsive to the clients — something which made it one of the most hideous monstrosities of Paris. Nay, were it not for the mouldy sacristies where prayers are weighed out and paid for like groceries, and for the old-clothes shops, where flutter the rags that blight all the illusions of life by showing us the last end of all our festivities — an attorney's office would be, of all social marts, the most loathsome. But we might say the same of the gambling-hell, of the Law Court, of the lottery office, of the brothel.

But why? In these places, perhaps, the drama being played in a man's soul makes him indifferent to accessories, which would also account for the single-mindedness of great thinkers and men of great ambitions.

'Where is my penknife?'

'I am eating my breakfast.'

'You go and be hanged! Here is a blot on the copy.'

'Silence, gentlemen!'

These various exclamations were uttered simultaneously at the moment when the old client shut the door with the sort of humility which disfigures the movements of a man down on his luck. The stranger tried to smile, but the muscles of his face relaxed as he vainly looked for some symptoms of amenity on the inexorably indifferent faces of the six clerks. Accustomed, no doubt, to gauge men, he very politely addressed the gutter-jumper, hoping to get a civil answer from this boy of all work.

'Monsieur, is your master at home?'

The pert messenger made no reply, but patted his ear with the fingers of his left hand, as much as to say, 'I am deaf.'

'What do you want, sir?' asked Godeschal, swallowing as he spoke a mouthful of bread big enough to charge a four-pounder, flourishing his knife and crossing his legs, throwing up one foot in the air to the level of his eyes.

'This is the fifth time I have called,' replied the victim. 'I wish to speak to M. Derville.'

'On business?'

'Yes, but I can explain it to no one but — '

'M. Derville is in bed; if you wish to consult him on some difficulty, he does no serious work till midnight. But if you will lay the case before us, we could help you just as well as he can to — '

The stranger was unmoved; he looked timidly about him, like a dog who has got into a strange kitchen and expects a kick. By grace of their profession, lawyers' clerks have no fear of thieves; they did not suspect the owner of the box-coat, and left him to study the place, where he looked in vain for a chair to sit on, for he was evidently tired. Attorneys, on principle, do not have many chairs in their offices. The inferior client, being kept waiting on his feet, goes away grumbling, but then he does not waste time, which, as an old lawyer once said, is not allowed for when the bill is taxed.

'Monsieur,' said the old man, 'as I have already told you, I cannot explain my business to any one but M. Derville. I will wait till he is up.'

Boucard had finished his bill. He smelt the fragrance of his chocolate, rose from his cane armchair, went to the chimney-piece, looked the old man from head to foot, stared at his coat, and made an indescribable grimace. He probably reflected that whichever way his client might be wrung, it would be impossible to squeeze out a centime, so he put in a few brief words to rid the office of a bad customer.

'It is the truth, monsieur. The chief only works at night. If your business is important, I recommend you to return at one in the morning.' The stranger looked at the head clerk with a bewildered expression, and remained motionless for a moment. The clerks, accustomed to every change of countenance, and the odd whimsicalities to which indecision or absence of mind gives rise in 'parties,' went on eating, making as much noise with their jaws as horses over a manger, and paying no further heed to the old man.

'I will come again to-night,' said the stranger at length, with the tenacious desire, peculiar to the unfortunate, to catch humanity at fault.

The only irony allowed to poverty is to drive Justice and Benevolence to unjust denials. When a poor wretch has convicted Society of falsehood, he throws himself more eagerly on the mercy of God.

'What do you think of that for a cracked pot?' said Simonnin, without waiting till the old man had shut the door.

'He looks as if he had been buried and dug up again,' said a clerk.

'He is some colonel who wants his arrears of pay,' said the head clerk.

'No, he is a retired concierge,' said Godeschal.

'I bet you he is a nobleman,' cried Boucard.

'I bet you he has been a porter,' retorted Godeschal. 'Only porters are gifted by nature with shabby box-coats, as worn and greasy and frayed as that old body's. And did you see his trodden-down boots that let the water in, and his stock which serves for a shirt? He has slept in a dry arch.'

'He may be of noble birth, and yet have pulled the doorlatch,' cried Desroches. 'It has been known!'

'No,' Boucard insisted, in the midst of laughter, 'I maintain that he was a brewer in 1789, and a colonel in the time of the Republic.'

'I bet theatre tickets round that he never was a soldier,' said Godeschal.

'Done with you,' answered Boucard.

'Monsieur! Monsieur!' shouted the little messenger, opening the window.

'What are you at now, Simonnin?' asked Boucard.

'I am calling him that you may ask him whether he is a colonel or a porter; he must know.'

All the clerks laughed. As to the old man, he was already coming upstairs again.

'What can we say to him?' cried Godeschal.

'Leave it to me,' replied Boucard.

The poor man came in nervously, his eyes cast down, perhaps not to betray how hungry he was by looking too greedily at the eatables.

'Monsieur,' said Boucard, 'will you have the kindness to leave your name, so that M. Derville may know — '

'Chabert.'

'The Colonel who was killed at Eylau?' asked Hure, who, having so far said nothing, was jealous of adding a jest to all the others.

'The same, monsieur,' replied the good man, with antique simplicity. And he went away.

'Whew!'

'Done brown!'

'Poof!'

'Oh!'

'Ah!'

'Boum!'

'The old rogue!'

'Ting-a-ring-ting!'

'Sold again!'

'Monsieur Desroches, you are going to the play without paying,' said Hure to the fourth clerk, giving him a slap on the shoulder that might have killed a rhinoceros.

There was a storm of cat-calls, cries, and exclamations, which all the onomatopeia of the language would fail to represent.

'Which theatre shall we go to?'

164

'To the opera,' cried the head clerk.

'In the first place,' said Godeschal, 'I never mentioned which theatre. I might, if I chose, take you to see Madame Saqui.'

'Madame Saqui is not the play.'

'What is a play?' replied Godeschal. 'First, we must define the point of fact. What did I bet, gentlemen? A play. What is a play? A spectacle. What is a spectacle? Something to be seen — '

'But on that principle you would pay your bet by taking us to see the water run under the Pont Neuf!' cried Simonnin, interrupting him.

'To be seen for money,' Godeschal added.

'But a great many things are to be seen for money that are not plays. The definition is defective,' said Desroches.

'But do listen to me!'

'You are talking nonsense, my dear boy,' said Boucard.

'Is Curtius' a play?' said Godeschal.

'No,' said the head clerk, 'it is a collection of figures — but it is a spectacle.'

'I bet you a hundred francs to a sou,' Godeschal resumed, 'that Curtius' Waxworks forms such a show as might be called a play or theatre. It contains a thing to be seen at various prices, according to the place you choose to occupy.'

'And so on, and so forth!' said Simonnin.

'You mind I don't box your ears!' said Godeschal.

The clerk shrugged their shoulders.

'Besides, it is not proved that that old ape was not making game of us,' he said, dropping his argument, which was drowned in the laughter of the other clerks. 'On my honor, Colonel Chabert is really and truly dead. His wife is married again to Comte Ferraud, Councillor of State. Madame Ferraud is one of our clients.'

'Come, the case is remanded till to-morrow,' said Boucard. 'To work, gentlemen. The deuce is in it; we get nothing done here. Finish copying that appeal; it must be handed in before the sitting of the Fourth Chamber, judgment is to be given to-day. Come, on you go!'

'If he really were Colonel Chabert, would not that impudent rascal Simonnin have felt the leather of his boot in the right place when he pretended to be deaf?' said Desroches, regarding this remark as more conclusive than Godeschal's.

'Since nothing is settled,' said Boucard, 'let us all agree to go to the upper boxes of the Francais and see Talma in 'Nero.' Simonnin may go to the pit.'

And thereupon the head clerk sat down at

his table, and the others followed his example.

'*Given in June eighteen hundred and fourteen* (in words),' said Godeschal. 'Ready?'

'Yes,' replied the two copying-clerks and the engrosser, whose pens forthwith began to creak over the stamped paper, making as much noise in the office as a hundred cockchafers imprisoned by schoolboys in paper cages.

'*And we hope that my lords on the Bench,*' the extemporizing clerk went on. 'Stop! I must read my sentence through again. I do not understand it myself.'

'Forty-six (that must often happen) and three forty-nines,' said Boucard.

'*We hope,*' Godeschal began again, after reading all through the document, '*that my lords on the Bench will not be less magnanimous than the august author of the decree, and that they will do justice against the miserable claims of the acting committee of the chief Board of the Legion of Honour by interpreting the law in the wide sense we have here set forth —* '

'Monsieur Godeschal, wouldn't you like a glass of water?' said the little messenger.

'That imp of a boy!' said Boucard. 'Here, get on your double-soled shanks-mare, take this packet, and spin off to the Invalides.'

'*Here set forth,*' Godeschal went on. 'Add

in the interest of *Madame la Vicomtesse* (at full length) *de Grandlieu.*'

'What!' cried the chief, 'are you thinking of drawing up an appeal in the case of Vicomtesse de Grandlieu against the Legion of Honour — a case for the office to stand or fall by? You are something like an ass! Have the goodness to put aside your copies and your notes; you may keep all that for the case of Navarreins against the Hospitals. It is late. I will draw up a little petition myself, with a due allowance of 'inasmuch,' and go to the Courts myself.'

This scene is typical of the thousand delights which, when we look back on our youth, make us say, 'Those were good times.'

At about one in the morning Colonel Chabert, self-styled, knocked at the door of Maitre Derville, attorney to the Court of First Instance in the Department of the Seine. The porter told him that Monsieur Derville had not yet come in. The old man said he had an appointment, and was shown upstairs to the rooms occupied by the famous lawyer, who, notwithstanding his youth, was considered to have one of the longest heads in Paris.

Having rung, the distrustful applicant was not a little astonished at finding the head clerk busily arranging in a convenient order

168

on his master's dining-room table the papers relating to the cases to be tried on the morrow. The clerk, not less astonished, bowed to the Colonel and begged him to take a seat, which the client did.

'On my word, monsieur, I thought you were joking yesterday when you named such an hour for an interview,' said the old man, with the forced mirth of a ruined man, who does his best to smile.

'The clerks were joking, but they were speaking the truth too,' replied the man, going on with his work. 'M. Derville chooses this hour for studying his cases, taking stock of their possibilities, arranging how to conduct them, deciding on the line of defence. His prodigious intellect is freer at this hour — the only time when he can have the silence and quiet needed for the conception of good ideas. Since he entered the profession, you are the third person to come to him for a consultation at this midnight hour. After coming in the chief will discuss each case, read everything, spend four or five hours perhaps over the business, then he will ring for me and explain to me his intentions. In the morning from ten to two he hears what his clients have to say, then he spends the rest of his day in appointments. In the evening he goes into society to keep up his connections. So he has only the night for undermining his cases, ransacking the arsenal of the code, and laying his plan of battle. He is determined never to lose a case; he loves his art. He will not undertake every case, as his brethren do. That is his life, an exceptionally active one. And he makes a great deal of money.'

As he listened to this explanation, the old man sat silent, and his strange face assumed an expression so bereft of intelligence, that the clerk, after looking at him, thought no more about him.

A few minutes later Derville came in, in evening dress; his head clerk opened the door to him, and went back to finish arranging the papers. The young lawyer paused for a moment in amazement on seeing in the dim light the strange client who awaited him. Colonel Chabert was as absolutely immovable as one of the wax figures in Curtius' collection to which Godeschal had proposed to treat his fellow-clerks. This quiescence would not have been a subject for astonishment if it had not completed the supernatural aspect of the man's whole person. The old soldier was dry and lean. His forehead, intentionally hidden under a smoothly combed wig, gave him a look of mystery. His eyes seemed shrouded in a transparent film; you would have compared them

to dingy mother-of-pearl with a blue irides-
cence changing in the gleam of the wax lights.
His face, pale, livid, and as thin as a knife, if I
may use such a vulgar expression, was as the
face of the dead. Round his neck was a tight
black silk stock.

Below the dark line of this rag the body was
so completely hidden in shadow that a man
of imagination might have supposed the old
head was due to some chance play of light
and shade, or have taken it for a portrait by
Rembrandt, without a frame. The brim of the
hat which covered the old man's brow cast a
black line of shadow on the upper part of the
face. This grotesque effect, though natural,
threw into relief by contrast the white
furrows, the cold wrinkles, the colourless tone
of the corpse-like countenance. And the
absence of all movement in the figure, of all
fire in the eye, were in harmony with a certain
look of melancholy madness, and the
deteriorating symptoms characteristic of
senility, giving the face an indescribably
ill-starred look which no human words could
render.

But an observer, especially a lawyer, could
also have read in this stricken man the signs
of deep sorrow, the traces of grief which had
worn into this face, as drops of water from
the sky falling on fine marble at last destroy

its beauty. A physician, an author, or a judge might have discerned a whole drama at the sight of its sublime horror, while the least charm was its resemblance to the grotesques which artists amuse themselves by sketching on a corner of the lithographic stone while chatting with a friend.

On seeing the attorney, the stranger started, with the convulsive thrill that comes over a poet when a sudden noise rouses him from a fruitful reverie in silence and at night. The old man hastily removed his hat and rose to bow to the young man; the leather lining of his hat was doubtless very greasy; his wig stuck to it without his noticing it, and left his head bare, showing his skull horribly disfigured by a scar beginning at the nape of the neck and ending over the right eye, a prominent seam all across his head. The sudden removal of the dirty wig which the poor man wore to hide this gash gave the two lawyers no inclination to laugh, so horrible to behold was this riven skull. The first idea suggested by the sight of this old wound was, 'His intelligence must have escaped through that cut.'

'If this is not Colonel Chabert, he is some thorough-going trooper!' thought Boucard.

'Monsieur,' said Derville, 'to whom have I the honour of speaking?'

'To Colonel Chabert.'

'Which?'

'He who was killed at Eylau,' replied the old man.

On hearing this strange speech, the lawyer and his clerk glanced at each other, as much as to say, 'He is mad.'

'Monsieur,' the Colonel went on, 'I wish to confide to you the secret of my position.'

A thing worthy of note is the natural intrepidity of lawyers. Whether from the habit of receiving a great many persons, or from the deep sense of the protection conferred on them by the law, or from confidence in their missions, they enter everywhere, fearing nothing, like priests and physicians. Derville signed to Boucard, who vanished.

'During the day, sir,' said the attorney, 'I am not so miserly of my time, but at night every minute is precious. So be brief and concise. Go to the facts without digression. I will ask for any explanations I may consider necessary. Speak.'

Having bid his strange client to be seated, the young man sat down at the table; but while he gave his attention to the deceased Colonel, he turned over the bundles of papers.

'You know, perhaps,' said the dead man, 'that I commanded a cavalry regiment at Eylau. I was of important service to the success of Murat's famous charge which decided the victory. Unhappily for me, my death is a historical fact, recorded in *Victoires et Conquetes*, where it is related in full detail. We cut through the three Russian lines, which at once closed up and formed again, so that we had to repeat the movement back again. At the moment when we were nearing the Emperor, after having scattered the Russians, I came against a squadron of the enemy's cavalry. I rushed at the obstinate brutes. Two Russian officers, perfect giants, attacked me both at once. One of them gave me a cut across the head that crashed through everything, even a black silk cap I wore next my head, and cut deep into the skull. I fell from my horse. Murat came up to support me. He rode over my body, he and all his men, fifteen hundred of them — there might have been more! My death was announced to the Emperor, who as a precaution — for he was fond of me, was the master — wished to know if there were no hope of saving the man he had to thank for such a vigorous attack. He sent two surgeons to identify me and bring me into Hospital, saying, perhaps too carelessly, for he was very busy, 'Go and see whether by any chance poor Chabert is still alive.' These rascally saw-bones, who had just seen me lying under the hoofs of the horses of two regiments, no doubt did not trouble themselves to feel my pulse, and reported that I was quite dead. The certificate of death was probably made out in accordance with the rules of military jurisprudence.'

As he heard his visitor express himself with complete lucidity, and relate a story so probable though so strange, the young lawyer ceased fingering the papers, rested his left elbow on the table, and with his head on his hand looked steadily at the Colonel.

'Do you know, monsieur, that I am lawyer to the Countess Ferraud,' he said, interrupting the speaker, 'Colonel Chabert's widow?'

'My wife — yes monsieur. Therefore, after a hundred fruitless attempts to interest lawyers, who have all thought me mad, I made up my mind to come to you. I will tell you of my misfortunes afterwards; for the present, allow me to prove the facts, explaining rather how things must have fallen out rather than how they did occur. Certain circumstances, known, I suppose to no one but the Almighty, compel me to speak of some things as hypothetical. The wounds I had received must presumably have produced tetanus, or have thrown me into a state analogous to that of a disease called, I believe, catalepsy. Otherwise how is it conceivable that I should have been stripped, as is the custom in time of the war, and thrown into the common grave by the men ordered to bury the dead?

'Allow me here to refer to a detail of which I could know nothing till after the event, which, after all, I must speak of as my death. At Stuttgart, in 1814, I met an old quartermaster of my regiment. This dear fellow, the only man who chose to recognize me, and of whom I will tell you more later, explained the marvel of my preservation, by telling me that my horse was shot in the flank at the moment when I was wounded. Man and beast went down together, like a monk cut out of card-paper. As I fell, to the right or to the left, I was no doubt covered by the body of my horse, which protected me from being trampled to death or hit by a ball.

'When I came to myself, monsieur, I was in a position and an atmosphere of which I could give you no idea if I talked till to-morrow. The little air there was to breathe was foul. I wanted to move, and found no room. I opened my eyes, and saw nothing. The most alarming circumstance was the lack of air, and this enlightened me as to my situation. I understood that no fresh air could penetrate to me, and that I must die. This thought took off the sense of intolerable pain which had aroused me. There was a violent singing in my ears. I heard — or I thought I heard, I will assert nothing — groans from the world of dead among whom I was lying. Some nights I still think I hear those stifled moans; though the remembrance of that time is very obscure, and my memory very indistinct, in spite of my impressions of far more acute suffering I was fated to go through, and which have confused my ideas.

'But there was something more awful than cries; there was a silence such as I have never known elsewhere — literally, the silence of the grave. At last, by raising my hands and feeling the dead, I discerned a vacant space between my head and the human carrion above. I could thus measure the space, granted by a chance of which I knew not the cause. It would seem that, thanks to the carelessness and the haste with which we had been pitched into the trench, two dead bodies had leaned across and against each other, forming an angle like that made by two cards when a child is building a card castle. Feeling about me at once, for there was no time for play, I happily felt an arm lying detached, the arm of a Hercules! A stout bone, to which I owed my rescue. But for this unhoped-for help, I must have perished. But with a fury you may imagine, I began to work my way through the bodies which separated me from the layer of earth which had no doubt been thrown over us — I say us, as if there had been others living! I worked with a will, monsieur, for here I am! But to this day I do not know how I succeeded in getting through the pile of flesh which formed a barrier between me and life. You will say I had three arms. This crowbar, which I used cleverly enough, opened out a little air between the bodies I moved, and I economized my breath. At last I saw daylight, but through snow!

'At that moment I perceived that my head was cut open. Happily my blood, or that of my comrades, or perhaps the torn skin of my horse, who knows, had in coagulating formed a sort of natural plaster. But, in spite of it, I fainted away when my head came into contact with the snow. However, the little warmth left in me melted the snow about me; and when I recovered consciousness, I found myself in the middle of a round hole, where I stood shouting as long as I could. But the sun was rising, so I had very little chance of being heard. Was there any one in the fields yet? I pulled myself up, using my feet as a spring, resting on one of the dead, whose ribs were firm. You may suppose that this was not the moment for saying, 'Respect courage in misfortune!' In short, monsieur, after enduring the anguish, if the word is strong enough for my frenzy, of seeing for a long time, yes, quite a long time, those cursed Germans flying from a voice they heard where they could see no one, I was dug out by a woman, who was brave or curious enough to come close to my head, which must have looked as though it had sprouted from the ground like a mushroom. This woman went to fetch her husband, and between them they got me to their poor hovel.

'It would seem that I must have again fallen into a catalepsy — allow me to use the word to describe a state of which I have no idea, but which, from the account given by my hosts, I suppose to have been the effect of that malady. I remained for six months between life and death; not speaking, or, if I spoke, talking in delirium. At last, my hosts got me admitted to the hospital at Heilsberg.

'You will understand, Monsieur, that I came out of the womb of the grave as naked as I came from my mother's; so that six months afterwards, when I remembered, one fine morning, that I had been Colonel Chabert, and when, on recovering my wits, I tried to exact from my nurse rather more respect than she paid to any poor devil, all my companions in the ward began to laugh. Luckily for me, the surgeon, out of professional pride, had answered for my cure, and was naturally interested in his patient. When I told him coherently about my former life, this good man, named Sparchmann, signed a deposition, drawn up in the legal form of his country, giving an account of the miraculous way in which I had escaped from the trench dug for the dead, the day and hour when I had been found by my benefactress and her husband, the nature and exact spot of my injuries, adding to these documents a description of my person.

'Well, monsieur, I have neither these important pieces of evidence, nor the declaration I made before a notary at Heilsberg, with a view to establishing my identity. From the day when I was turned out of that town by the events of the war, I have wandered about like a vagabond, begging my bread, treated as a madman when I have told my story, without ever having found or earned a sou to enable me to recover the deeds which would prove my statements, and restore me to society. My sufferings have often kept me for six months at a time in some little town, where every care was taken of the invalid Frenchman, but where he was laughed at to his face as soon as he said he was Colonel Chabert. For a long time that laughter, those doubts, used to put me into rages which did me harm, and which even led to my being locked up at Stuttgart as a madman. And indeed, as you may judge from my story, there was ample reason for shutting a man up.

'At the end of two years' detention, which I was compelled to submit to, after hearing my keepers say a thousand times, 'Here is a poor man who thinks he is Colonel Chabert' to people who would reply, 'Poor fellow!' I became convinced of the impossibility of my own adventure. I grew melancholy, resigned, and quiet, and gave up calling myself Colonel Chabert, in order to get out of my prison, and see France once more. Oh, monsieur! To see Paris again was a delirium which I — '

Without finishing his sentence, Colonel Chabert fell into a deep study, which Derville respected.

'One fine day,' his visitor resumed, 'one spring day, they gave me the key of the fields, as we say, and ten thalers, admitting that I talked quite sensibly on all subjects, and no longer called myself Colonel Chabert. On my honour, at that time, and even to this day, sometimes I hate my name. I wish I were not myself. The sense of my rights kills me. If my illness had but deprived me of all memory of my past life, I could be happy. I should have entered the service again under any name, no matter what, and should, perhaps, have been made Field-Marshal in Austria or Russia. Who knows?'

'Monsieur,' said the attorney, 'you have upset all my ideas. I feel as if I heard you in a dream. Pause for a moment, I beg of you.'

'You are the only person,' said the Colonel, with a melancholy look, 'who ever listened to me so patiently. No lawyer has been willing to lend me ten napoleons to enable me to procure from Germany the necessary documents to begin my lawsuit — '

'What lawsuit?' said the attorney, who had forgotten his client's painful position in listening to the narrative of his past sufferings.

'Why, monsieur, is not the Comtesse Ferraud my wife? She has thirty thousand francs a year, which belong to me, and she will not give me a son. When I tell lawyers these things — men of sense; when I propose — I, a beggar — to bring action against a Count and Countess; when I — a dead man — bring up as against a certificate of death a certificate of marriage and registers of births, they show me out, either with the air of cold politeness, which you all know how to assume to rid yourself of a hapless wretch, or brutally, like men who think they have to deal with a swindler or a madman — it depends on their nature. I have been buried under the dead;

but now I am buried under the living, under papers, under facts, under the whole of society, which wants to shove me underground again!'

'Pray resume your narrative,' said Derville.

"Pray resume it!" cried the hapless old man, taking the young lawyer's hand. 'That is the first polite word I have heard since — '

The Colonel wept. Gratitude choked his voice. The appealing and unutterable eloquence that lies in the eyes, in a gesture, even in silence, entirely convinced Derville, and touched him deeply.

'Listen, monsieur,' said he; 'I have this evening won three hundred francs at cards. I may very well lay out half that sum in making a man happy. I will begin the inquiries and researches necessary to obtain the documents of which you speak, and until they arrive I will give you five francs a day. If you are Colonel Chabert, you will pardon the smallness of the loan as it is coming from a young man who has his fortune to make. Proceed.'

The Colonel, as he called himself, sat for a moment motionless and bewildered; the depth of his woes had no doubt destroyed his powers of belief. Though he was eager in pursuit of his military distinction, of his fortune, of himself, perhaps it was in obedience to the inexplicable feeling, the latent germ in every man's heart, to which we owe the experiments of alchemists, the passion for glory, the discoveries of astronomy and of physics, everything which prompts man to expand his being by multiplying himself through deeds or ideas. In his mind the *Ego* was now but a secondary object, just as the vanity of success or the pleasures of winning become dearer to the gambler than the object he has at stake. The young lawyer's words were as a miracle to this man, for ten years repudiated by his wife, by justice, by the whole social creation. To find in a lawyer's office the ten gold pieces which had so long been refused him by so many people, and in so many ways! The colonel was like the lady who, having been ill of a fever for fifteen years, fancied she had some fresh complaint when she was cured. There are joys in which we have ceased to believe; they fall on us, it is like a thunderbolt; they burn us. The poor man's gratitude was too great to find utterance. To superficial observers he seemed cold, but Derville saw complete honesty under this amazement. A swindler would have found his voice.

'Where was I?' said the Colonel, with the simplicity of a child or of a soldier, for there is often something of the child in a true soldier, and almost always something of the soldier in a child, especially in France.

'At Stuttgart. You were out of prison,' said Derville.

'You know my wife?' asked the Colonel.

'Yes,' said Derville, with a bow.

'What is she like?'

'Still quite charming.'

The old man held up his hand, and seemed to be swallowing down some secret anguish with the grave and solemn resignation that is characteristic of men who have stood the ordeal of blood and fire on the battlefield.

'Monsieur,' said he, with a sort of cheerfulness — for he breathed again, the poor Colonel; he had again risen from the grave; he had just melted a covering of snow less easily thawed than that which had once before frozen his head; and he drew a deep breath, as if he had just escaped from a dungeon — 'Monsieur, if I had been a handsome young fellow, none of my misfortunes would have befallen me. Women believe in men when they flavour their speeches with the word Love. They hurry then, they come, they go, they are everywhere at once; they intrigue, they assert facts, they play the very devil for a man who takes their fancy. But how could I interest a woman? I had a face like a Requiem. I was dressed like a *sansculotte*. I was more like an Esquimaux than a Frenchman — I, who had formerly been considered one of the smartest of fops in 1799! — I, Chabert, Count of the Empire.

'Well, on the very day when I was turned out into the streets like a dog, I met the quartermaster of whom I just now spoke. This old soldier's name was Boutin. The poor devil and I made the queerest pair of broken-down hacks I ever set eyes on. I met him out walking; but though I recognized him, he could not possibly guess who I was. We went into a tavern together. In there, when I told him my name, Boutin's mouth opened from ear to ear in a roar of laughter, like the bursting of a mortar. That mirth, monsieur, was one of the keenest pangs I have known. It told me without disguise how great were the changes in me! I was, then, unrecognizable even to the humblest and most grateful of my former friends!

'I had once saved Boutin's life, but it was only the repayment of a debt I owed him. I need not tell you how he did me this service; it was at Ravenna, in Italy. The house where Boutin prevented my being stabbed was not extremely respectable. At that time I was not a colonel, but, like Boutin himself, a common trooper. Happily there were certain details of this adventure which could be known only to us two, and when I recalled them to his mind his incredulity diminished. I then told him the story of my singular experiences. Although my eyes and my voice, he told me, were strangely altered, although I had neither hair, teeth, nor eyebrows, and was as colourless as an Albino, he at last recognized his Colonel in the beggar, after a thousand questions, which I answered triumphantly.

'He related his adventures; they were not less extraordinary than my own; he had lately come back from the frontiers of China, which he had tried to cross after escaping from Siberia. He told me of the catastrophe of the Russian campaign, and of Napoleon's first abdication. That news was one of the things which caused me most anguish!

'We were two curious derelicts, having been rolled over the globe as pebbles are rolled by the ocean when storms bear them from shore to shore. Between us we had seen Egypt, Syria, Spain, Russia, Holland, Germany, Italy and Dalmatia, England, China, Tartary, Siberia; the only thing wanting was that neither of us had been to America or the Indies. Finally, Boutin, who still was more locomotive than I, undertook to go to Paris as quickly as might be to inform my wife of the predicament in which I was. I wrote a long letter full of details to Madame Chabert. That, monsieur, was the fourth! If I had had any relations, perhaps nothing of all this might have happened; but, to be frank with you, I am but a workhouse child, a soldier, whose sole fortune was his courage, whose sole family is mankind at large, whose country is France, whose only protector is the Almighty. — Nay, I am wrong! I had a father — the Emperor! Ah! if he were but here, the dear man! If he could see *his Chabert*, as he used to call me, in the state in which I am now, he would be in a rage! What is to be done? Our sun is set, and we are all out in the cold now. After all, political events might account for my wife's silence!

'Boutin set out. He was a lucky fellow! He had two bears, admirably trained, which brought him in a living. I could not go with him; the pain I suffered forbade my walking long stages. I wept, monsieur, when we parted, after I had gone as far as my state allowed in company with him and his bears. At Carlsruhe I had an attack of neuralgia in the head, and lay for six weeks on straw in an inn. I should never have ended if I were to tell you all the distresses of my life as a beggar. Moral suffering, before which physical suffering pales, nevertheless excites less pity, because it is not seen. I remember shedding tears, as I stood in front of a fine house in Strassburg where once I had given an entertainment, and where nothing was given me, not even a piece of bread. Having agreed with Boutin on the road I was to take, I went to every post-office to ask if there were a letter or some money for me. I arrived at Paris without having found either. What despair I had been forced to endure! 'Boutin must be dead!' I told myself, and in fact the poor fellow was killed at Waterloo. I heard of his death later, and by mere chance. His errand to my wife had, of course, been fruitless.

'At last I entered Paris — with the Cossacks. To me this was grief on grief. On seeing the Russians in France, I quite forgot that I had no shoes on my feet nor money in my pocket. Yes, monsieur, my clothes were in tatters. The evening before I reached Paris I was obliged to bivouac in the woods of Claye. The chill of the night air no doubt brought on an attack of some nameless complaint which seized me as I was crossing the Faubourg Saint-Martin. I dropped almost senseless at the door of an ironmonger's shop. When I recovered I was in a bed in the Hotel-Dieu. There I stayed very contentedly for about a month. I was then turned out; I had no money, but I was well, and my feet were on the good stones of Paris. With what delight and haste did I make my way to the Rue du Mont-Blanc, where my wife should be living in a house belonging to me! Bah! the Rue du Mont-Blanc was now the Rue de la Chausee d'Antin; I could not find my house; it had been sold and pulled down. Speculators had built several houses over my gardens. Not knowing that my wife had married M. Ferraud, I could obtain no information.

'At last I went to the house of an old lawyer who had been in charge of my affairs. This worthy man was dead, after selling his connection to a younger man. This gentleman informed me, to my great surprise, of the administration of my estate, the settlement of the moneys, of my wife's marriage, and the birth of her two children. When I told him that I was Colonel Chabert, he laughed so heartily that I left him without saying another word. My detention at Stuttgart had suggested possibilities of Charenton, and I determined to act with caution. Then, monsieur, knowing where my wife lived, I went to her house, my heart high with hope. — Well,' said the Colonel, with a gesture of concentrated fury, 'when I called under an assumed name I was not admitted, and on the day when I used my own I was turned out of doors.

'To see the Countess come home from a ball or the play in the early morning, I have sat whole nights through, crouching close to the wall of her gateway. My eyes pierced the depths of the carriage, which flashed past me with the swiftness of lightning, and I caught a glimpse of the woman who is my wife and no longer mine. Oh, from that day I have lived for vengeance!' cried the old man in a hollow voice, and suddenly standing up in front of Derville. 'She knows that I am alive; since my return she has had two letters written with my own hand. She loves me no more! — I — I know not whether I love or hate her. I long for her and curse her by turns. To me she owes all her fortune, all her happiness; well, she has not sent me the very smallest pittance. Sometimes I do not know what will become of me!'

With these words the veteran dropped on to his chair again and remained motionless. Derville sat in silence, studying his client.

'It is a serious business,' he said at length, mechanically. 'Even granting the genuineness of the documents to be procured from Heilsberg, it is not proved to me that we can at once win our case. It must go before three tribunals in succession. I must think such a matter over with a clear head; it is quite exceptional.'

'Oh,' said the Colonel, coldly, with a haughty jerk of his head, 'if I fail, I can die — but not alone.'

The feeble old man had vanished. The eyes were those of a man of energy, lighted up with the spark of desire and revenge.

'We must perhaps compromise,' said the lawyer.

'Compromise!' echoed Colonel Chabert. 'Am I dead, or am I alive?'

'I hope, monsieur,' the attorney went on, 'that you will follow my advice. Your cause is mine. You will soon perceive the interest I take in your situation, almost unexampled in judicial records. For the moment I will give you a letter to my notary, who will pay to your order fifty francs every ten days. It would be unbecoming for you to come here to receive alms. If you are Colonel Chabert, you ought to be at no man's mercy. I shall record these advances as a loan; you have estates to recover; you are rich.'

This delicate compassion brought tears to the old man's eyes. Derville rose hastily, for it was perhaps not correct for a lawyer to show emotion; he went into the adjoining room, and came back with an unsealed letter, which he gave to the Colonel. When the poor man held it in his hand, he felt through the paper two gold pieces.

'Will you be good enough to describe the documents, and tell me the name of the town, and in what kingdom?' said the lawyer.

The Colonel dictated the information, and verified the spelling of the names of places; then he took his hat in one hand, looked at Derville, and held out the other — a horny hand, saying with much simplicity:

'On my honour, sir, after the Emperor, you are the man to whom I shall owe most. You are a splendid fellow!'

The attorney clapped his hand into the Colonel's, saw him to the stairs, and held a light for him.

'Boucard,' said Derville to his head clerk, 'I have just listened to a tale that may cost me five and twenty louis. If I am robbed, I shall not regret the money, for I shall have seen the most consummate actor of the day.'

When the Colonel was in the street and close to a lamp, he took the two twenty-franc pieces out of the letter and looked at them for a moment under the light. It was the first gold he had seen for nine years.

'I may smoke cigars!' he said to himself.

About three months after this interview, at night, in Derville's room, the notary commissioned to advance the half-pay on Derville's account to his eccentric client, came to consult the attorney on a serious matter, and began by begging him to refund the six hundred francs that the old soldier had received.

'Are you amusing yourself with pensioning

the old army?' said the notary, laughing — a young man named Crottat, who had just bought up the office in which he had been head clerk, his chief having fled in consequence of a disastrous bankruptcy.

'I have to thank you, my dear sir, for reminding me of that affair,' replied Derville. 'My philanthropy will not carry me beyond twenty-five louis; I have, I fear, already been the dupe of my patriotism.'

As Derville finished the sentence, he saw on his desk the papers his head clerk had laid out for him. His eye was struck by the appearance of the stamps — long, square, and triangular, in red and blue ink, which distinguished a letter that had come through the Prussian, Austrian, Bavarian, and French post-offices.

'Ah ha!' said he with a laugh, 'here is the last act of the comedy; now we shall see if I have been taken in!'

He took up the letter and opened it; but he could not read it; it was written in German.

'Boucard, go yourself and have this letter translated, and bring it back immediately,' said Derville, half opening his study door, and giving the letter to the head clerk.

The notary at Berlin, to whom the lawyer had written, informed him that the documents he had been requested to forward would arrive within a few days of this note announcing them. They were, he said, all perfectly regular and duly witnessed, and legally stamped to serve as evidence in law. He also informed him that almost all the witnesses to the facts recorded under these affidavits were still to be found at Eylau, in Prussia, and that the woman to whom M. le Comte Chabert owed his life was still living in a suburb of Heilsberg.

'This looks like business,' cried Derville, when Boucard had given him the substance of the letter. 'But look here, my boy,' he went on, addressing the notary, 'I shall want some information which ought to exist in your office. Was it not that old rascal Roguin — ?'

'We will say that unfortunate, that ill-used Roguin,' interrupted Alexandre Crottat with a laugh.

'Well, was it not that ill-used man who has just carried off eight hundred thousand francs of his clients' money, and reduced several families to despair, who effected the settlement of Chabert's estate? I fancy I have seen that in the documents in our case of Ferraud.'

'Yes,' said Crottat. 'It was when I was third clerk; I copied the papers and studied them thoroughly. Rose Chapotel, wife and widow of Hyacinthe, called Chabert, Count of the Empire, grand officer of the Legion of Honor.

They had married without settlement; thus, they held all the property in common. To the best of my recollections, the personalty was about six hundred thousand francs. Before his marriage, Colonel Chabert had made a will in favour of the hospitals of Paris, by which he left them one-quarter of the fortune he might possess at the time of his decease, the State to take the other quarter. The will was contested, there was a forced sale, and then a division, for the attorneys went at a pace. At the time of the settlement the monster who was then governing France handed over to the widow, by special decree, the portion bequeathed to the treasury.'

'So that Comte Chabert's personal fortune was no more than three hundred thousand francs?'

'Consequently so it was, old fellow!' said Crottat. 'You lawyers sometimes are very clear-headed, though you are accused of false practices in pleading for one side or the other.'

Colonel Chabert, whose address was written at the bottom of the first receipt he had given the notary, was lodging in the Faubourg Saint-Marceau, Rue du Petit-Banquier, with an old quartermaster of the Imperial Guard, now a cowkeeper, named Vergniaud. Having reached the spot, Derville was obliged to go on foot in search of his client, for his coachman declined to drive along an unpaved street, where the ruts were rather too deep for cab wheels. Looking about him on all sides, the lawyer at last discovered at the end of the street nearest to the boulevard, between two walls built of bones and mud, two shabby stone gate-posts, much knocked about by carts, in spite of two wooden stumps that served as blocks. These posts supported a cross beam with a penthouse coping of tiles, and on the beam, in red letters, were the words, 'Vergniaud, dairyman.' To the right of this inscription were some eggs, to the left a cow, all painted in white. The gate was open, and no doubt remained open all day. Beyond a good-sized yard there was a house facing the gate, if indeed the name of house may be applied to one of the hovels built in the neighbourhood of Paris, which are like nothing else, not even the most wretched dwellings in the country, of which they have all the poverty without their poetry.

Indeed, in the midst of the fields, even a hovel may have a certain grace derived from the pure air, the verdure, the open country — a hill, a serpentine road, vineyards, quickset hedges, moss-grown thatch and rural implements; but poverty in Paris gains dignity

197

only by horror. Though recently built, this house seemed ready to fall into ruins. None of its materials had found a legitimate use; they had been collected from the various demolitions which are going on every day in Paris. On a shutter made of the boards of a shop-sign Derville read the words, 'Fancy Goods.' The windows were all mismatched and grotesquely placed. The ground floor, which seemed to be the habitable part, was on one side raised above the soil, and on the other sunk in the rising ground. Between the gate and the house lay a puddle full of stable litter, into which flowed the rain-water and house waste. The back wall of this frail construction, which seemed rather more solidly built than the rest, supported a row of barred hutches, where rabbits bred their numerous families. To the right of the gate was the cowhouse, with a loft above for fodder; it communicated with the house through the dairy. To the left was a poultry yard, with a stable and pigsties, the roofs finished, like that of the house, with rough deal boards nailed so as to overlap, and shabbily thatched with rushes.

Like most of the places where the elements of the huge meal daily devoured by Paris are every day prepared, the yard Derville now entered showed traces of the hurry that comes of the necessity for being ready at a fixed hour. The large pot-bellied tin cans in which milk is carried, and the little pots for cream, were flung pell-mell at the dairy door, with their linen-covered stoppers. The rags that were used to clean them, fluttered in the sunshine, riddled with holes, hanging to strings fastened to poles. The placid horse, of a breed known only to milk-women, had gone a few steps from the cart, and was standing in front of the stable, the door being shut. A goat was munching the shoots of a starved and dusty vine that clung to the cracked yellow wall of the house. A cat, squatting on the cream jars, was licking them over. The fowls, scared by Derville's approach, scuttered away screaming, and the watch-dog barked.

'And the man who decided the victory at Eylau is to be found here!' said Derville to himself, as his eyes took in at a glance the general effect of the squalid scene.

The house had been left in charge of three little boys. One, who had climbed to the top of the cart loaded with hay, was pitching stones into the chimney of a neighbouring house, in the hope that they might fall into a saucepan; another was trying to get a pig into a cart, to hoist it by making the whole thing tilt. When Derville asked them if M. Chabert lived there, neither of them replied, but all three looked at him with a sort of bright stupidity, if I may combine those two words. Derville repeated his questions, but without success. Provoked by the saucy cunning of these three imps, he abused them with the sort of pleasantry which young men think they have the right to address to little boys, and they broke the silence with a horse-laugh. Then Derville was angry.

The Colonel, hearing him, now came out of the little low room, close to the dairy, and stood on the threshold of his doorway with indescribable military coolness. He had in his mouth a very finely-coloured pipe — a technical phrase to a smoker — a humble, short clay pipe of the kind called 'brule-queule.' He lifted the peak of a dreadfully greasy cloth cap, saw Derville, and came straight across the midden to join his benefactor the sooner, calling out in friendly tones to the boys:

'Silence in the ranks!'

The children at once kept a respectful silence, which showed the power the old soldier had over them.

'Why did you not write to me?' he said to Derville. 'Go along by the cowhouse! There — the path is paved there,' he exclaimed, seeing the lawyer's hesitancy, for he did not wish to wet his feet in the manure heap.

Jumping from one dry spot to another, Derville reached the door by which the Colonel had come out. Chabert seemed but ill pleased at having to receive him in the bed-room he occupied; and, in fact, Derville found but one chair there. The Colonel's bed consisted of some trusses of straw, over which his hostess had spread two or three of those old fragments of carpet, picked up heaven knows where, which milk-women use to cover the seats of their carts. The floor was simply the trodden earth. The walls, sweating salt-petre, green with mould, and full of cracks, were so excessively damp that on the side where the Colonel's bed was a reed mat had been nailed. The famous box-coat hung on a nail. Two pairs of old boots lay in a corner. There was not a sign of linen. On the worm-eaten table the *Bulletins de la Grande Armee*, reprinted by Plancher, lay open, and seemed to be the Colonel's reading; his countenance was calm and serene in the midst of this squalor. His visit to Derville seemed to have altered his features; the lawyer perceived in them traces of a happy feeling, a particular gleam set there by hope.

'Does the smell of the pipe annoy you?' he said, placing the dilapidated straw-bottomed chair for his lawyer.

'But, Colonel, you are dreadfully uncomfortable here!'

The speech was wrung from Derville by the distrust natural to lawyers, and the deplorable experience which they derive early in life from the appalling and obscure tragedies at which they look on.

'Here,' said he to himself, 'is a man who has of course spent my money in satisfying a trooper's three theological virtues — play, wine, and women!'

'To be sure, monsieur, we are not distinguished for luxury here. It is a camp lodging, tempered by friendship, but — ' And the soldier shot a deep glance at the man of law — 'I have done no one wrong, I have never turned my back on anybody, and I sleep in peace.'

Derville reflected that there would be some want of delicacy in asking his client to account for the sums of money he had advanced, so he merely said:

'But why would you not come to Paris, where you might have lived as cheaply as you do here, but where you would have been better lodged?'

'Why,' replied the Colonel, 'the good folks with whom I am living had taken me in and fed me *gratis* for a year. How could I leave them just when I had a little money? Besides, the father of those three pickles is an old *Egyptian* — '

'An Egyptian!'

'We give that name to the troopers who came back from the expedition into Egypt, of which I was one. Not merely are all who get back brothers; Vergniaud was in my regiment. We have shared a draught of water in the desert; and besides, I have not yet finished teaching his brats to read.'

'He might have lodged you better for your money,' said Derville.

'Bah!' said the Colonel, 'his children sleep on the straw as I do. He and his wife have no better bed; they are very poor you see. They have taken a bigger business than they can manage. But if I recover my fortune . . . However, it does very well.'

'Colonel, to-morrow or the next day, I shall receive your papers from Heilsberg. The woman who dug you out is still alive!'

'Curse the money! To think I haven't got any!' he cried, flinging his pipe on the ground.

Now, a well-coloured pipe is to a smoker a precious possession; but the impulse was so natural, the emotion so generous, that every smoker, and the excise office itself, would have pardoned this crime of treason to tobacco. Perhaps the angels may have picked up the pieces.

'Colonel, it is an exceedingly complicated business,' said Derville as they left the room to walk up and down in the sunshine.

'To me,' said the soldier, 'it appears exceedingly simple. I was thought to be dead, and here I am! Give me back my wife and my fortune; give me the rank of General, to which I have a right, for I was made Colonel of the Imperial Guard the day before the battle of Eylau.'

'Things are not done so in the legal world,' said Derville. 'Listen to me. You are Colonel Chabert, I am glad to think it; but it has to be proved judicially to persons whose interest it will be to deny it. Hence, your papers will be disputed. That contention will give rise to ten or twelve preliminary inquiries. Every question will be sent under contradiction up to the supreme court, and give rise to so many costly suits, which will hang on for a long time, however eagerly I may push them. Your opponents will demand an inquiry, which we cannot refuse, and which may necessitate the sending of a commission of investigation to Prussia. But even if we hope for the best; supposing that justice should at once recognize you as Colonel Chabert — can we know how the questions will be settled that will arise out of the very innocent bigamy committed by the Comtesse Ferraud?

'In your case, the point of law is unknown to the Code, and can only be decided as a point in equity, as a jury decides in the delicate cases presented by the social eccentricities of some criminal prosecutions. Now, you had no children by your marriage; M. le Comte Ferraud has two. The judges might pronounce against the marriage where the family ties are weakest, to the confirmation of that where they are stronger, since it was contracted in perfect good faith. Would you be in a very becoming moral position if you insisted, at your age, and in your present circumstances, in resuming your rights over a woman who no longer loves you? You will have both your wife and her husband against you, two important persons who might influence the Bench. Thus, there are many elements which would prolong the case; you will have time to grow old in the bitterest regrets.'

'And my fortune?'

'Do you suppose you had a fine fortune?'

'Had I not thirty thousand francs a year?'

'My dear Colonel, in 1799 you made a will before your marriage, leaving one-quarter of your property to hospitals.'

'That is true.'

'Well, when you were reported dead, it was necessary to make a valuation, and have a sale, to give this quarter away. Your wife was not particular about honesty as to the poor. The valuation, in which she no doubt took care not to include the ready money or jewellery, or too much of the plate, and in which the furniture would be estimated at two-thirds of its actual cost, either to benefit her, or to lighten the succession duty, and also because a valuer can be held responsible for the declared value — the valuation thus made stood at six hundred thousand francs. Your wife had a right of half for her share. Everything was sold and bought in by her; she got something out of it all, and the hospitals got their seventy-five thousand francs. Then, as the remainder went to the State, since you had made no mention of your wife in your will, the Emperor restored to your widow by decree the residue which would have reverted to the Exchequer. So, now, what can you claim? Three hundred thousand francs, no more, and minus the costs.'

'And you call that justice!' said the Colonel, in dismay.

'Why, certainly — '

'A pretty kind of justice!'

'So it is, my dear Colonel. You see, that what you thought so easy is not so. Madame Ferraud might even choose to keep the sum given to her by the Emperor.'

'But she was not a widow. The decree is utterly void — '

'I agree with you. But every case can get a hearing. Listen to me. I think that under these circumstances a compromise would be both for her and for you the best solution of the question. You will gain by it a more considerable sum than you can prove a right to.'

'That would be to sell my wife!'

'With twenty-four thousand francs a year you could find a woman who, in the position in which you are, would suit you better than your own wife, and make you happier. I propose going this very day to see the Comtesse Ferraud and sounding the ground; but I would not take such a step without giving you due notice.'

'Let us go together.'

'What, just as you are?' said the lawyer. 'No, my dear Colonel, no. You might lose your case on the spot.'

'Can I possibly gain it?'

'On every count,' replied Derville. 'But, my dear Colonel Chabert, you overlook one thing. I am not rich; the price of my connection is not wholly paid up. If the bench should allow you a maintenance, that is to say, a sum advanced on your prospects, they will not do so till you have proved that you are Comte Chabert, grand officer of the Legion of Honor.'

'To be sure, I am a grand officer of the Legion of Honor; I had forgotten that,' said he simply.

'Well, until then,' Derville went on, 'will you not have to engage pleaders, to have documents copied, to keep the underlings of the law going, and to support yourself? The expenses of the preliminary inquiries will, at a rough guess, amount to ten or twelve thousand francs. I have not so much to lend you — I am crushed as it is by the enormous interest I have to pay on the money I borrowed to buy my business; and you? — Where can you find it?'

Large tears gathered in the poor veteran's faded eyes, and rolled down his withered cheeks. This outlook of difficulties discouraged him. The social and the legal world weighed on his breast like a nightmare.

'I will go to the foot of the Vendome column!' he cried. 'I will call out: 'I am Colonel Chabert who rode through the Russian square at Eylau!' — The statue — he — he will know me.'

'And you will find yourself in Charenton.'

At this terrible name the soldier's transports collapsed.

'And will there be no hope for me at the Ministry of War?'

'The war office!' said Derville. 'Well, go there; but take a formal legal opinion with you, nullifying the certificate of your death. The government offices would be only too glad if they could annihilate the men of the Empire.'

The Colonel stood for a while, speechless, motionless, his eyes fixed, but seeing nothing, sunk in bottomless despair. Military justice is ready and swift; it decides with Turklike finality, and almost always rightly. This was the only justice known to Chabert. As he saw the labyrinth of difficulties into which he must plunge, and how much money would be required for the journey, the poor old soldier was mortally hit in that power peculiar to man, and called the Will. He thought it would be impossible to live as party to a lawsuit; it seemed a thousand times simpler to remain poor and a beggar, or to enlist as a trooper if any regiment would pass him.

His physical and mental sufferings had already impaired his bodily health in some of the most important organs. He was on the verge of one of those maladies for which medicine has no name, and of which the seat is in some degree variable, like the nervous system itself, the part most frequently attacked of the whole human machine, a malady which may be designated as the heart-sickness of the unfortunate. However serious this invisible but real disorder might already be, it could still be cured by a happy issue. But a fresh obstacle, an unexpected incident, would be enough to wreck this vigorous constitution, to break the weakened springs, and produce the hesitancy, the aimless, unfinished movements, which physiologists know well in men undermined by grief.

Derville, detecting in his client the symptoms of extreme dejection, said to him:

'Take courage; the end of the business cannot fail to be in your favour. Only, consider whether you can give me your whole confidence and blindly accept the result I may think best for your interests.'

'Do what you will,' said Chabert.

'Yes, but you surrender yourself to me like a man marching to his death.'

'Must I not be left to live without a position, without a name? Is that endurable?'

'That is not my view of it,' said the lawyer. 'We will try a friendly suit, to annul both your death certificate and your marriage, so as to put you in possession of your rights. You may even, by Comte Ferraud's intervention, have your name replaced on the army list as general, and no doubt you will get a pension.'

'Well, proceed then,' said Chabert. 'I put myself entirely in your hands.'

'I will send you a power of attorney to sign,' said Derville. 'Good-bye. Keep up your courage. If you want money, rely on me.'

Chabert warmly wrung the lawyer's hand, and remained standing with his back against the wall, not having the energy to follow him excepting with his eyes. Like all men who know but little of legal matters, he was frightened by this unforeseen struggle.

During their interview, several times, the figure of a man posted in the street had come forward from behind one of the gate-pillars, watching for Derville to depart, and he now accosted the lawyer. He was an old man, wearing a blue waistcoat and a white-pleated kilt, like a brewer's; on his head was an otter-skin cap. His face was tanned, hollow-cheeked, and wrinkled, but ruddy on the cheek-bones by hard work and exposure to the open air.

'Asking your pardon, sir,' said he, taking Derville by the arm, 'if I take the liberty of speaking to you. But I fancied, from the look of you, that you were a friend of our General's.'

'And what then?' replied Derville. 'What concern have you with him? — But who are you?' said the cautious lawyer.

'I am Louis Vergniaud,' he replied at once. 'I have a few words to say to you.'

'So you are the man who has lodged Comte Chabert as I have found him?'

'Asking your pardon, sir, he has the best room. I would have given him mine if I had had but one; I could have slept in the stable. A man who has suffered as he has, who teaches my kids to read, a general, an Egyptian, the first lieutenant I ever served under — What do you think? — Of us all, he is best served. I shared what I had with him. Unfortunately, it is not much to boast of — bread, milk, eggs. Well, well; it's neighbours' fare, sir. And he is heartily welcome. — But he has hurt our feelings.'

'He?'

'Yes, sir, hurt our feelings. To be plain with you, I have taken a larger business than I can manage, and he saw it. Well, it worried him; he must needs mind the horse! I says to him, 'Really, General — ' 'Bah!' says he, 'I am not going to eat my head off doing nothing. I learned to rub a horse down many a year ago.' — I had some bills out for the purchase money of my dairy — a fellow named Grados — Do you know him, sir?'

'But, my good man, I have not time to listen to your story. Only tell me how the

Colonel offended you.'

'He hurt our feelings, sir, as sure as my name is Louis Vergniaud, and my wife cried about it. He heard from our neighbours that we had not a sou to begin to meet the bills with. The old soldier, as he is, he saved up all you gave him, he watched for the bill to come in, and he paid it. Such a trick! While my wife and me, we knew he had no tobacco, poor old boy, and went without. — Oh! now — yes, he has his cigar every morning! I would sell my soul for it — No, we are hurt. Well, so I wanted to ask you — for he said you were a good sort — to lend us a hundred crowns on the stock, so that we may get him some clothes, and furnish his room. He thought he was getting us out of debt, you see? Well, it's just the other way; the old man is running us into debt — and hurt our feelings! — He ought not to have stolen a march on us like that. And we his friends, too! — On my word as an honest man, as sure as my name is Louis Vergniaud, I would sooner sell up and enlist than fail to pay you back your money — '

Derville looked at the dairyman, and stepped back a few paces to glance at the house, the yard, the manure-pool, the cowhouse, the rabbits, the children.

'On my honour, I believe it is characteristic

of virtue to have nothing to do with riches!'
thought he.

'All right, you shall have your hundred
crowns, and more. But I shall not give them
to you; the Colonel will be rich enough to
help, and I will not deprive him of the
pleasure.'

'And will that be soon?'

'Why, yes.'

'Ah, dear God! how glad my wife will be!'
and the cowkeeper's tanned face seemed to
expand.

'Now,' said Derville to himself, as he got
into his cab again, 'let us call on our
opponent. We must not show our hand, but
try to see hers, and win the game at one
stroke. She must be frightened. She is a
woman. Now, what frightens women most? A
woman is afraid of nothing but . . . '

And he set to work to study the Countess'
position, falling into one of those brown
studies to which great politicians give
themselves up when concocting their own
plans and trying to guess the secrets of a
hostile Cabinet. Are not attorneys, in a way,
statesmen in charge of private affairs?

But a brief survey of the situation in which
the Comte Ferraud and his wife now found
themselves is necessary for a comprehension
of the lawyer's cleverness.

Monsieur le Comte Ferraud was the only son of a former Councillor in the old *Parlement* of Paris, who had emigrated during the Reign of Terror, and so, though he saved his head, lost his fortune. He came back under the Consulate, and remained persistently faithful to the cause of Louis XVIII., in whose circle his father had moved before the Revolution. He thus was one of the party in the Faubourg Saint-Germain which nobly stood out against Napoleon's blandishments. The reputation for capacity gained by the young Count — then simply called Monsieur Ferraud — made him the object of the Emperor's advances, for he was often as well pleased at his conquests among the aristocracy as at gaining a battle. The Count was promised the restitution of his title, of such of his estates as had not been sold, and he was shown in perspective a place in the ministry or as senator.

The Emperor fell.

At the time of Comte Chabert's death, M. Ferraud was a young man of six-and-twenty, without a fortune, of pleasing appearance, who had had his successes, and whom the Faubourg Saint-Germain had adopted as doing it credit; but Madame la Comtesse Chabert had managed to turn her share of her husband's fortune to such good account that, after eighteen months of widowhood, she had about forty thousand francs a year. Her marriage to the young Count was not regarded as news in the circles of the Faubourg Saint-Germain. Napoleon, approving of this union, which carried out his idea of fusion, restored to Madame Chabert the money falling to the Exchequer under her husband's will; but Napoleon's hopes were again disappointed. Madame Ferraud was not only in love with her lover; she had also been fascinated by the notion of getting into the haughty society which, in spite of its humiliation, was still predominant at the Imperial Court. By this marriage all her vanities were as much gratified as her passions. She was to become a real fine lady. When the Faubourg Saint-Germain understood that the young Count's marriage did not mean desertion, its drawing-rooms were thrown open to his wife.

Then came the Restoration. The Count's political advancement was not rapid. He understood the exigencies of the situation in which Louis XVIII. found himself; he was one of the inner circle who waited till the 'Gulf of Revolution should be closed' — for this phrase of the King's, at which the Liberals laughed so heartily, had a political sense. The order quoted in the long lawyer's preamble at the beginning of this story had, however, put him in possession of two tracts of forest, and of an estate which had considerably increased in value during its sequestration. At the present moment, though Comte Ferraud was a Councillor of State, and a Director-General, he regarded his position as merely the first step of his political career.

Wholly occupied as he was by the anxieties of consuming ambition, he had attached to himself, as secretary, a ruined attorney named Delbecq, a more than clever man, versed in all the resources of the law, to whom he left the conduct of his private affairs. This shrewd practitioner had so well understood his position with the Count as to be honest in his own interest. He hoped to get some place by his master's influence, and he made the Count's fortune his first care. His conduct so effectually gave the lie to his former life, that he was regarded as a slandered man. The Countess, with the tact and shrewdness of which most women have a share more or less, understood the man's motives, watched him quietly, and managed him so well, that she had made good use of him for the augmentation of her private fortune. She had contrived to make Delbecq believe that she ruled her husband, and had promised to get him appointed President of an inferior court in some important provincial town, if he devoted himself entirely to her interests.

The promise of a place, not dependent on changes of ministry, which would allow of his marrying advantageously, and rising subsequently to a high political position, by being chosen Depute, made Delbecq the Countess' abject slave. He had never allowed her to miss one of those favourable chances which the fluctuations of the Bourse and the increased value of property afforded to clever financiers in Paris during the first three years after the Restoration. He had trebled his protectress' capital, and all the more easily because the Countess had no scruples as to the means which might make her an enormous fortune as quickly as possible. The emoluments derived by the Count from the places he held she spent on the housekeeping, so as to reinvest her dividends; and Delbecq lent himself to these calculations of avarice without trying to account for her motives. People of that sort never trouble themselves about any secrets of which the discovery is not necessary to their own interests. And, indeed, he naturally found the reason in the thirst for money, which taints almost every Parisian woman; and as a fine fortune was needed to support the pretensions of Comte Ferraud, the secretary sometimes fancied that he saw in the Countess' greed a consequence of her devotion to a husband with whom she still was in love. The Countess buried the secrets of her conduct at the bottom of her heart. There lay the secrets of life and death to her, there lay the turning-point of this history.

At the beginning of the year 1818 the Restoration was settled on an apparently immovable foundation; its doctrines of government, as understood by lofty minds, seemed calculated to bring to France an era of renewed prosperity, and Parisian society changed its aspect. Madame la Comtesse Ferraud found that by chance she had achieved for love a marriage that had brought her fortune and gratified ambition. Still young and handsome, Madame Ferraud played the part of a woman of fashion, and lived in the atmosphere of the Court. Rich herself, with a rich husband who was cried up as one of the ablest men of the royalist party, and, as a friend of the King, certain to be made Minister, she belonged to the aristocracy, and shared its magnificence. In the midst of this triumph she was attacked by a moral canker. There are feelings which women guess in spite of the care men take to bury them. On the first return of the King, Comte Ferraud had begun to regret his marriage. Colonel Chabert's widow had not been the means of allying him to anybody; he was alone and unsupported in steering his way in a course full of shoals and beset by enemies. Also, perhaps, when he came to judge his wife coolly, he may have discerned in her certain vices of education which made her unfit to second him in his schemes.

A speech he made, a propos of Talleyrand's marriage, enlightened the Countess, to whom it proved that if he had still been a free man she would never have been Madame Ferraud. What woman could forgive this repentance? Does it not include the germs of every insult, every crime, every form of repudiation? But what a wound must it have left in the Countess' heart, supposing that she lived in the dread of her first husband's return? She had known that he still lived, and she had ignored him. Then during the time when she had heard no more of him, she had chosen to believe that he had fallen at Waterloo with the Imperial Eagle, at the same time as Boutin. She resolved, nevertheless, to bind the Count to her by the strongest of all ties, by a chain of gold, and vowed to be so rich that her fortune might make her second marriage dissoluble, if by chance Colonel Chabert should ever reappear. And he had reappeared; and she could not explain to herself why the struggle she had dreaded had not already begun. Suffering, sickness, had perhaps delivered her from that man. Perhaps he was half mad, and Charenton might yet do her justice. She had not chosen to take either Delbecq or the police into her confidence, for fear of putting herself in their power, or of hastening the catastrophe. There are in Paris many women who, like the Countess Ferraud, live with an unknown moral monster, or on the brink of an abyss; a callus forms over the spot that tortures them, and they can still laugh and enjoy themselves.

'There is something very strange in Comte Ferraud's position,' said Derville to himself, on emerging from his long reverie, as his cab stopped at the door of the Hotel Ferraud in the Rue de Varennes. 'How is it that he, so rich as he is, and such a favorited with the King, is not yet a peer of France? It may, to be sure, be true that the King, as Mme. de Grandlieu was telling me, desires to keep up the value of the *pairie* by not bestowing it right and left. And, after all, the son of a Councillor of the *Parlement* is not a Crillon nor a Rohan. A Comte Ferraud can only get into the Upper Chamber surreptitiously. But if his marriage were annulled, could he not get the dignity of some old peer who has only daughters transferred to himself, to the King's great satisfaction? At any rate this will be a good bogey to put forward and frighten the Countess,' thought he as he went up the steps.

Derville had without knowing it laid his finger on the hidden wound, put his hand on the canker that consumed Madame Ferraud.

She received him in a pretty winter dining-room, where she was at breakfast, while playing with a monkey tethered by a chain to a little pole with climbing bars of iron. The Countess was in an elegant wrapper; the curls of her hair, carelessly pinned up, escaped from a cap, giving her an arch look. She was fresh and smiling. Silver, gilding, and mother-of-pearl shone on the table, and all about the room were rare plants growing in magnificent china jars. As he saw Colonel Chabert's wife, rich with his spoil, in the lap of luxury and the height of fashion, while he, poor wretch, was living with a poor dairyman among the beasts, the lawyer said to himself:

'The moral of all this is that a pretty woman will never acknowledge as her husband, nor even as a lover, a man in an old box-coat, a tow wig, and boots with holes in them.'

A mischievous and bitter smile expressed

the feelings, half philosophical and half satirical, which such a man was certain to experience — a man well situated to know the truth of things in spite of the lies behind which most families in Paris hide their mode of life.

'Good-morning, Monsieur Derville,' said she, giving the monkey some coffee to drink.

'Madame,' said he, a little sharply, for the light tone in which she spoke jarred on him. 'I have come to speak with you on a very serious matter.'

'I am so *grieved*, M. le Comte is away — '

'I, madame, am delighted. It would be grievous if he could be present at our interview. Besides, I am informed through M. Delbecq that you like to manage your own business without troubling the Count.'

'Then I will send for Delbecq,' said she.

'He would be of no use to you, clever as he is,' replied Derville. 'Listen to me, madame; one word will be enough to make you grave. Colonel Chabert is alive!'

'Is it by telling me such nonsense as that that you think you can make me grave?' said she with a shout of laughter. But she was suddenly quelled by the singular penetration of the fixed gaze which Derville turned on her, seeming to read to the bottom of her soul.

'Madame,' he said with cold and piercing solemnity, 'you know not the extent of the danger that threatens you. I need say nothing of the indisputable authenticity of the evidence nor of the fullness of proof which testifies to the identity of Comte Chabert. I am not, as you know, the man to take up a bad cause. If you resist our proceedings to show that the certificate of death was false, you will lose that first case, and that matter once settled, we shall gain every point.'

'What, then, do you wish to discuss with me?'

'Neither the Colonel nor yourself. Nor need I allude to the briefs which clever advocates may draw up when armed with the curious facts of this case, or the advantage they may derive from the letters you received from your first husband before your marriage to your second.'

'It is false,' she cried, with the violence of a spoilt woman. 'I never had a letter from Comte Chabert; and if some one is pretending to be the Colonel, it is some swindler, some returned convict, like Coignard perhaps. It makes me shudder only to think of it. Can the Colonel rise from the dead, monsieur? Bonaparte sent an aide-de-camp to inquire for me on his death, and to this day I draw the pension of three thousand francs granted to this widow by the Government. I have been perfectly in the right to turn away all the Chaberts who have ever come, as I shall all who may come.'

'Happily we are alone, madame. We can tell lies at our ease,' said he coolly, and finding it amusing to lash up the Countess' rage so as to lead her to betray herself, by tactics familiar to lawyers, who are accustomed to keep cool when their opponents or their clients are in a passion. 'Well, then, we must fight it out,' thought he, instantly hitting on a plan to entrap her and show her her weakness.

'The proof that you received the first letter, madame, is that it contained some securities — '

'Oh, as to securities — that it certainly did not.'

'Then you received the letter,' said Derville, smiling. 'You are caught, madame, in the first snare laid for you by an attorney, and you fancy you could fight against Justice — '

The Countess coloured, and then turned pale, hiding her face in her hands. Then she shook off her shame, and retorted with the natural impertinence of such women, 'Since you are the so-called Chabert's attorney, be so good as to — '

'Madame,' said Derville, 'I am at this

moment as much your lawyer as I am Colonel Chabert's. Do you suppose I want to lose so valuable a client as you are? — But you are not listening.'

'Nay, speak on, monsieur,' said she graciously.

'Your fortune came to you from M. le Comte Chabert, and you cast him off. Your fortune is immense, and you leave him to beg. An advocate can be very eloquent when a cause is eloquent in itself; there are here circumstances which might turn public opinion strongly against you.'

'But, monsieur,' said the Comtesse, provoked by the way in which Derville turned and laid her on the gridiron, 'even if I grant that your M. Chabert is living, the law will uphold my second marriage on account of the children, and I shall get off with the restitution of two hundred and twenty-five thousand francs to M. Chabert.'

'It is impossible to foresee what view the Bench may take of the question. If on one side we have a mother and children, on the other we have an old man crushed by sorrows, made old by your refusals to know him. Where is he to find a wife? Can the judges contravene the law? Your marriage with Colonel Chabert has priority on its side and every legal right. But if you appear under disgraceful colours, you might have an unlooked-for adversary. That, madame, is the danger against which I would warn you.'

'And who is he?'

'Comte Ferraud.'

'Monsieur Ferraud has too great an affection for me, too much respect for the mother of his children — '

'Do not talk of such absurd things,' interrupted Derville, 'to lawyers, who are accustomed to read hearts to the bottom. At this instant Monsieur Ferraud has not the slightest wish to annul your union, and I am quite sure that he adores you; but if some one were to tell him that his marriage is void, that his wife will be called before the bar of public opinion as a criminal — '

'He would defend me, monsieur.'

'No, madame.'

'What reason could he have for deserting me, monsieur?'

'That he would be free to marry the only daughter of a peer of France, whose title would be conferred on him by patent from the King.'

The Countess turned pale.

'A hit!' said Derville to himself. 'I have you on the hip; the poor Colonel's case is won.' — 'Besides, madame,' he went on aloud, 'he would feel all the less remorse because a man covered with glory — a General, Count, Grand Cross of the Legion of Honor — is not such a bad alternative; and if that man insisted on his wife's returning to him — '

'Enough, enough, monsieur!' she exclaimed. 'I will never have any lawyer but you. What is to be done?'

'Compromise!' said Derville.

'Does he still love me?' she said.

'Well, I do not think he can do otherwise.'

The Countess raised her head at these words. A flash of hope shone in her eyes; she thought perhaps that she could speculate on her first husband's affection to gain her cause by some feminine cunning.

'I shall await your orders, madame, to know whether I am to report our proceedings to you, or if you will come to my office to agree to the terms of a compromise,' said Derville, taking leave.

A week after Derville had paid these two visits, on a fine morning in June, the husband and wife, who had been separated by an almost supernatural chance, started from the opposite ends of Paris to meet in the office of the lawyer who was engaged by both. The supplies liberally advanced by Derville to Colonel Chabert had enabled him to dress as suited his position in life, and the dead man arrived in a very decent cab. He wore a wig suited to his face, was dressed in blue cloth with white linen, and wore under his waistcoat the broad red ribbon of the higher grade of the Legion of Honor. In resuming the habits of wealth he had recovered his soldierly style. He held himself up; his face, grave and mysterious-looking, reflected his happiness and all his hopes, and seemed to have acquired youth and *impasto*, to borrow a picturesque word from the painter's art. He was no more like the Chabert of the old box-coat than a cartwheel double sou is like a newly coined forty-franc piece. The passer-by, only to see him, would have recognized at once one of the noble wrecks of our old army, one of the heroic men on whom our national glory is reflected, as a splinter of ice on which the sun shines seems to reflect every beam. These veterans are at once a picture and a book.

When the Count jumped out of his carriage to go into Derville's office, he did it as lightly as a young man. Hardly had his cab moved off, when a smart brougham drove up, splendid with coats-of-arms. Madame la Comtesse Ferraud stepped out in a dress which, though simple, was cleverly designed to show how youthful her figure was. She wore a pretty drawn bonnet lined with pink, which framed her face to perfection, softening its outlines and making it look younger.

If the clients were rejuvenescent, the office was unaltered, and presented the same picture as that described at the beginning of this story. Simonnin was eating his breakfast, his shoulder leaning against the window, which was then open, and he was staring up at the blue sky in the opening of the courtyard enclosed by four gloomy houses.

'Ah, ha!' cried the little clerk, 'who will bet an evening at the play that Colonel Chabert is a General, and wears a red ribbon?'

'The chief is a great magician,' said Godeschal.

'Then there is no trick to play on him this time?' asked Desroches.

'His wife has taken that in hand, the Comtesse Ferraud,' said Boucard.

'What next?' said Godeschal. 'Is Comtesse Ferraud required to belong to two men?'

'Here she is,' answered Simonnin.

'So you are not deaf, you young rogue!' said Chabert, taking the gutter-jumper by the ear and twisting it, to the delight of the other clerks, who began to laugh, looking at the Colonel with the curious attention due to so singular a personage.

Comte Chabert was in Derville's private room at the moment when his wife came in by the door of the office.

'I say, Boucard, there is going to be a queer scene in the chief's room! There is a woman who can spend her days alternately, the odd with Comte Ferraud, and the even with Comte Chabert.'

'And in leap year,' said Godeschal, 'they must settle the *count* between them.'

'Silence, gentlemen, you can be heard!' said Boucard severely. 'I never was in an office where there was so much jesting as there is here over the clients.'

Derville had made the Colonel retire to the bedroom when the Countess was admitted.

'Madame,' he said, 'not knowing whether it would be agreeable to you to meet M. le Comte Chabert, I have placed you apart. If, however, you should wish it — '

'It is an attention for which I am obliged to you.'

'I have drawn up the memorandum of an agreement of which you and M. Chabert can discuss the conditions, here, and now. I will go alternately to him and to you, and explain your views respectively.'

'Let me see, monsieur,' said the Countess impatiently.

Derville read aloud:

''Between the undersigned:

''M. Hyacinthe Chabert, Count, Marechal de Camp, and Grand Officer of the Legion of

231

Honor, living in Paris, Rue du Petit-Banquier, on the one part;

''And Madame Rose Chapotel, wife of the aforesaid M. le Comte Chabert, *nee* — ''

'Pass over the preliminaries,' said she. 'Come to the conditions.'

'Madame,' said the lawyer, 'the preamble briefly sets forth the position in which you stand to each other. Then, by the first clause, you acknowledge, in the presence of three witnesses, of whom two shall be notaries, and one the dairyman with whom your husband has been lodging, to all of whom your secret is known, and who will be absolutely silent — you acknowledge, I say, that the individual designated in the documents subjoined to the deed, and whose identity is to be further proved by an act of recognition prepared by your notary, Alexandre Crottat, is your first husband, Comte Chabert. By the second clause Comte Chabert, to secure your happiness, will undertake to assert his rights only under certain circumstances set forth in the deed. — And these,' said Derville, in a parenthesis, 'are none other than a failure to carry out the conditions of this secret agreement. — M. Chabert, on his part, agrees to accept judgment on a friendly suit, by which his certificate of death shall be annulled, and his marriage dissolved.'

'That will not suit me in the least,' said the Countess with surprise. 'I will be a party to no suit; you know why.'

'By the third clause,' Derville went on, with imperturbable coolness, 'you pledge yourself to secure to Hyacinthe Comte Chabert an income of twenty-four thousand francs on government stock held in his name, to revert to you at his death — '

'But it is much too dear!' exclaimed the Countess.

'Can you compromise the matter cheaper?'

'Possibly.'

'But what do you want, madame?'

'I want — I will not have a lawsuit. I want — '

'You want him to remain dead?' said Derville, interrupting her hastily.

'Monsieur,' said the Countess, 'if twenty-four thousand francs a year are necessary, we will go to law — '

'Yes, we will go to law,' said the Colonel in a deep voice, as he opened the door and stood before his wife, with one hand in his waistcoat and the other hanging by his side — an attitude to which the recollection of his adventure gave horrible significance.

'It is he,' said the Countess to herself.

'Too dear!' the old soldier exclaimed. 'I have given you near on a million, and you are cheapening my misfortunes. Very well; now I will have you — you and your fortune. Our goods are in common, our marriage is not dissolved — '

'But monsieur is not Colonel Chabert!' cried the Countess, in feigned amazement.

'Indeed!' said the old man, in a tone of intense irony. 'Do you want proofs? I found you in the Palais Royal — '

The Countess turned pale. Seeing her grow white under her rouge, the old soldier paused, touched by the acute suffering he was inflicting on the woman he had once so ardently loved; but she shot such a venomous glance at him that he abruptly went on:

'You were with La — '

'Allow me, Monsieur Derville,' said the Countess to the lawyer. 'You must give me leave to retire. I did not come here to listen to such dreadful things.'

She rose and went out. Derville rushed after her; but the Countess had taken wings, and seemed to have flown from the place.

On returning to his private room, he found the Colonel in a towering rage, striding up and down.

'In those times a man took his wife where he chose,' said he. 'But I was foolish and chose badly; I trusted to appearances. She has no heart.'

'Well, Colonel, was I not right to beg you not to come? — I am now positive of your identity; when you came in, the Countess gave a little start, of which the meaning was unequivocal. But you have lost your chances. Your wife knows that you are unrecognizable.'

'I will kill her!'

'Madness! you will be caught and executed like any common wretch. Besides you might miss! That would be unpardonable. A man must not miss his shot when he wants to kill his wife. — Let me set things straight; you are only a big child. Go now. Take care of yourself; she is capable of setting some trap for you and shutting you up in Charenton. I will notify her of our proceedings to protect you against a surprise.'

The unhappy Colonel obeyed his young benefactor, and went away, stammering apologies. He slowly went down the dark staircase, lost in gloomy thoughts, and crushed perhaps by the blow just dealt him — the most cruel he could feel, the thrust that could most deeply pierce his heart — when he heard the rustle of a woman's dress on the lowest landing, and his wife stood before him.

'Come, monsieur,' said she, taking his arm with a gesture like those familiar to him of old. Her action and the accent of her voice, which had recovered its graciousness, were enough to allay the Colonel's wrath, and he allowed himself to be led to the carriage.

'Well, get in!' said she, when the footman had let down the step.

And as if by magic, he found himself sitting by his wife in the brougham.

'Where to?' asked the servant.

'To Groslay,' said she.

The horses started at once, and carried them all across Paris.

'Monsieur,' said the Countess, in a tone of voice which betrayed one of those emotions which are rare in our lives, and which agitate every part of our being. At such moments the heart, fibres, nerves, countenance, soul, and body, everything, every pore even, feels a thrill. Life no longer seems to be within us; it flows out, springs forth, is communicated as if by contagion, transmitted by a look, a tone of voice, a gesture, impressing our will on others. The old soldier started on hearing this single word, this first, terrible 'monsieur!' But still it was at once a reproach and a pardon, a hope and a despair, a question and an answer. This word included them all; none but an actress could have thrown so much eloquence, so many feelings into a single word. Truth is less complete in its utterance; it does not put everything on the outside; it allows us to see what is within. The Colonel was filled with remorse for his suspicions, his demands, and his anger; he looked down not to betray his agitation.

'Monsieur,' repeated she, after an imperceptible pause, 'I knew you at once.'

'Rosine,' said the old soldier, 'those words contain the only balm that can help me to forget my misfortunes.'

Two large tears rolled hot on to his wife's hands, which he pressed to show his paternal affection.

'Monsieur,' she went on, 'could you not have guessed what it cost me to appear before a stranger in a position so false as mine now is? If I have to blush for it, at least let it be in the privacy of my family. Ought not such a secret to remain buried in our hearts? You will forgive me, I hope, for my apparent indifference to the woes of a Chabert in whose existence I could not possibly believe. I received your letters,' she hastily added, seeing in his face the objection it expressed, 'but they did not reach me till thirteen months after the battle of Eylau. They were opened, dirty, the writing was unrecognizable; and after obtaining Napoleon's signature to my second marriage contract, I could not help believing that some clever swindler wanted to make a fool of me. Therefore, to avoid disturbing Monsieur Ferraud's peace of mind, and disturbing family ties, I was obliged to take precautions against a pretended Chabert. Was I not right, I ask you?'

'Yes, you were right. It was I who was the idiot, the owl, the dolt, not to have calculated better what the consequences of such a position might be. — But where are we going?' he asked, seeing that they had reached the barrier of La Chapelle.

'To my country house near Groslay, in the valley of Montmorency. There, monsieur, we will consider the steps to be taken. I know my duties. Though I am yours by right, I am no longer yours in fact. Can you wish that we should become the talk of Paris? We need not inform the public of a situation, which for me has its ridiculous side, and let us preserve our dignity. You still love me,' she said, with a sad, sweet gaze at the Colonel, 'but have not I been authorized to form other ties? In so strange a position, a secret voice bids me trust to your kindness, which is so well known to me. Can I be wrong in taking you as the sole arbiter of my fate? Be at once judge and party to the suit. I trust in your noble character; you will be generous enough to forgive me for the consequences of faults committed in innocence. I may then confess to you: I love M. Ferraud. I believed that I had a right to love him. I do not blush to make this confession to you; even if it offends you, it does not disgrace us. I cannot conceal the facts. When fate made me a widow, I was not a mother.'

The Colonel with a wave of his hand bid his wife be silent, and for a mile and a half they sat without speaking a single word. Chabert could fancy he saw the two little ones before him.

'Rosine.'

'Monsieur?'

'The dead are very wrong to come to life again.'

'Oh, monsieur, no, no! Do not think me ungrateful. Only, you find me a lover, a mother, while you left me merely a wife. Though it is no longer in my power to love, I know how much I owe you, and I can still offer you all the affection of a daughter.'

'Rosine,' said the old man in a softened tone, 'I no longer feel any resentment against you. We will forget anything,' he added, with one of those smiles which always reflect a noble soul; 'I have not so little delicacy as to demand the mockery of love from a wife who no longer loves me.'

The Countess gave him a flashing look full of such deep gratitude that poor Chabert would have been glad to sink again into his grave at Eylau. Some men have a soul strong enough for such self-devotion, of which the whole reward consists in the assurance that they have made the person they love happy.

'My dear friend, we will talk all this over later when our hearts have rested,' said the Countess.

The conversation turned to other subjects, for it was impossible to dwell very long on this one. Though the couple came back again and again to their singular position, either by some allusion or of serious purpose, they had a delightful drive, recalling the events of their former life together and the times of the Empire. The Countess knew how to lend peculiar charm to her reminiscences, and gave the conversation the tinge of melancholy that was needed to keep it serious. She revived his love without awakening his desires, and allowed her first husband to discern the mental wealth she had acquired while trying to accustom him to moderate his pleasure to that which a father may feel in the society of a favorited daughter.

The Colonel had known the Countess of the Empire; he found her a Countess of the Restoration.

At last, by a cross-road, they arrived at the entrance to a large park lying in the little valley which divides the heights of Margency from the pretty village of Groslay. The

Countess had there a delightful house, where the Colonel on arriving found everything in readiness for his stay there, as well as for his wife's. Misfortune is a kind of talisman whose virtue consists in its power to confirm our original nature; in some men it increases their distrust and malignancy, just as it improves the goodness of those who have a kind heart.

Sorrow had made the Colonel even more helpful and good than he had always been, and he could understand some secrets of womanly distress which are unrevealed to most men. Nevertheless, in spite of his loyal trustfulness, he could not help saying to his wife:

'Then you felt quite sure you would bring me here?'

'Yes,' replied she, 'if I found Colonel Chabert in Derville's client.'

The appearance of truth she contrived to give to this answer dissipated the slight suspicions which the Colonel was ashamed to have felt. For three days the Countess was quite charming to her first husband. By tender attentions and unfailing sweetness she seemed anxious to wipe out the memory of the sufferings he had endured, and to earn forgiveness for the woes which, as she confessed, she had innocently caused him. She delighted in displaying for him the charms she knew he took pleasure in, while at the same time she assumed a kind of melancholy; for men are more especially accessible to certain ways, certain graces of the heart or of the mind which they cannot resist. She aimed at interesting him in her position, and appealing to his feelings so far as to take possession of his mind and control him despotically.

Ready for anything to attain her ends, she did not yet know what she was to do with this man; but at any rate she meant to annihilate him socially. On the evening of the third day she felt that in spite of her efforts she could not conceal her uneasiness as to the results of her manoeuvres. To give herself a minute's reprieve she went up to her room, sat down before her writing-table, and laid aside the mask of composure which she wore in Chabert's presence, like an actress who, returning to her dressing-room after a fatiguing fifth act, drops half dead, leaving with the audience an image of herself which she no longer resembles. She proceeded to finish a letter she had begun to Delbecq, whom she desired to go in her name and demand of Derville the deeds relating to Colonel Chabert, to copy them, and to come to her at once to Groslay. She had hardly finished when she heard the Colonel's step in the passage; uneasy at her absence, he had come to look for her.

'Alas!' she exclaimed, 'I wish I were dead! My position is intolerable . . . '

'Why, what is the matter?' asked the good man.

'Nothing, nothing!' she replied.

She rose, left the Colonel, and went down to speak privately to her maid, whom she sent off to Paris, impressing on her that she was herself to deliver to Delbecq the letter just written, and to bring it back to the writer as soon as he had read it. Then the Countess went out to sit on a bench sufficiently in sight for the Colonel to join her as soon as he might choose. The Colonel, who was looking for her, hastened up and sat down by her.

'Rosine,' said he, 'what is the matter with you?'

She did not answer.

It was one of those glorious, calm evenings in the month of June, whose secret harmonies infuse such sweetness into the sunset. The air was clear, the stillness perfect, so that far away in the park they could hear the voices of some children, which added a kind of melody to the sublimity of the scene.

'You do not answer me?' the Colonel said to his wife.

'My husband — ' said the Countess, who

broke off, started a little, and with a blush stopped to ask him, 'What am I to say when I speak of M. Ferraud?'

'Call him your husband, my poor child,' replied the Colonel, in a kind voice. 'Is he not the father of your children?'

'Well, then,' she said, 'if he should ask what I came here for, if he finds out that I came here, alone, with a stranger, what am I to say to him? Listen, monsieur,' she went on, assuming a dignified attitude, 'decide my fate, I am resigned to anything — '

'My dear,' said the Colonel, taking possession of his wife's hands, 'I have made up my mind to sacrifice myself entirely for your happiness — '

'That is impossible!' she exclaimed, with a sudden spasmodic movement. 'Remember that you would have to renounce your identity, and in an authenticated form.'

'What?' said the Colonel. 'Is not my word enough for you?'

The word 'authenticated' fell on the old man's heart, and roused involuntary distrust. He looked at his wife in a way that made her colour, she cast down her eyes, and he feared that he might find himself compelled to despise her. The Countess was afraid lest she had scared the shy modesty, the stern honesty, of a man whose generous temper and primitive virtues were known to her. Though these feelings had brought the clouds to her brow, they immediately recovered their harmony. This was the way of it. A child's cry was heard in the distance.

'Jules, leave your sister in peace,' the Countess called out.

'What, are your children here?' said Chabert.

'Yes, but I told them not to trouble you.'

The old soldier understood the delicacy, the womanly tact of so gracious a precaution, and took the Countess' hand to kiss it.

'But let them come,' said he.

The little girl ran up to complain of her brother.

'Mamma!'

'Mamma!'

'It was Jules — '

'It was her — '

Their little hands were held out to their mother, and the two childish voices mingled; it was an unexpected and charming picture.

'Poor little things!' cried the Countess, no longer restraining her tears, 'I shall have to leave them. To whom will the law assign them? A mother's heart cannot be divided; I want them, I want them.'

'Are you making mamma cry?' said Jules, looking fiercely at the Colonel.

'Silence, Jules!' said the mother in a decided tone.

The two children stood speechless, examining their mother and the stranger with a curiosity which it is impossible to express in words.

'Oh yes!' she cried. 'If I am separated from the Count, only leave me my children, and I will submit to anything . . .'

This was the decisive speech which gained all that she had hoped from it.

'Yes,' exclaimed the Colonel, as if he were ending a sentence already begun in his mind, 'I must return underground again. I had told myself so already.'

'Can I accept such a sacrifice?' replied his wife. 'If some men have died to save a mistress' honour, they gave their life but once. But in this case you would be giving your life every day. No, no. It is impossible. If it were only your life, it would be nothing; but to sign a declaration that you are not Colonel Chabert, to acknowledge yourself an imposter, to sacrifice your honour, and live a lie every hour of the day! Human devotion cannot go so far. Only think! — No. But for my poor children I would have fled with you by this time to the other end of the world.'

'But,' said Chabert, 'cannot I live here in your little lodge as one of your relations? I am as worn out as a cracked cannon; I want nothing but a little tobacco and the *Constitutionnel*.'

The Countess melted into tears. There was a contest of generosity between the Comtesse Ferraud and Colonel Chabert, and the soldier came out victorious. One evening, seeing this mother with her children, the soldier was bewitched by the touching grace of a family picture in the country, in the shade and the silence; he made a resolution to remain dead, and, frightened no longer at the authentication of a deed, he asked what he could do to secure beyond all risk the happiness of this family.

'Do exactly as you like,' said the Countess. 'I declare to you that I will have nothing to do with this affair. I ought not.'

Delbecq had arrived some days before, and in obedience to the Countess' verbal instructions, the intendant had succeeded in gaining the old soldier's confidence. So on the following morning Colonel Chabert went with the erewhile attorney to Saint-Leu-Taverny, where Delbecq had caused the notary to draw up an affidavit in such terms that, after hearing it read, the Colonel started up and walked out of the office.

'Turf and thunder! What a fool you must think me! Why, I should make myself out a swindler!' he exclaimed.

'Indeed, monsieur,' said Delbecq, 'I should advise you not to sign in haste. In your place I would get at least thirty thousand francs a year out of the bargain. Madame would pay them.'

After annihilating this scoundrel *emeritus* by the lightning look of an honest man insulted, the Colonel rushed off, carried away by a thousand contrary emotions. He was suspicious, indignant, and calm again by turns.

Finally he made his way back into the park of Groslay by a gap in a fence, and slowly walked on to sit down and rest, and meditate at his ease, in a little room under a gazebo, from which the road to Saint-Leu could be seen. The path being strewn with the yellowish sand which is used instead of river-gravel, the Countess, who was sitting in the upper room of this little summer-house, did not hear the Colonel's approach, for she was too much preoccupied with the success of her business to pay the smallest attention to the slight noise made by her husband. Nor did the old man notice that his wife was in the room over him.

'Well, Monsieur Delbecq, has he signed?' the Countess asked her secretary, whom she saw alone on the road beyond the hedge of a haha.

'No, madame. I do not even know what has become of our man. The old horse reared.'

'Then we shall be obliged to put him into Charenton,' said she, 'since we have got him.'

The Colonel, who recovered the elasticity of youth to leap the haha, in the twinkling of an eye was standing in front of Delbecq, on whom he bestowed the two finest slaps that ever a scoundrel's cheeks received.

'And you may add that old horses can kick!' said he.

His rage spent, the Colonel no longer felt vigorous enough to leap the ditch. He had seen the truth in all its nakedness. The Countess' speech and Delbecq's reply had revealed the conspiracy of which he was to be the victim. The care taken of him was but a bait to entrap him in a snare. That speech was like a drop of subtle poison, bringing on in the old soldier a return of all his sufferings, physical and moral. He came back to the summer-house through the park gate, walking slowly like a broken man.

Then for him there was to be neither peace nor truce. From this moment he must begin the odious warfare with this woman of which Derville had spoken, enter on a life of litigation, feed on gall, drink every morning of the cup of bitterness. And then — fearful thought! — where was he to find the money needful to pay the cost of the first proceedings? He felt such disgust of life, that if there had been any water at hand he would have thrown himself into it; that if he had had a pistol, he would have blown out his brains. Then he relapsed into the indecision of mind which, since his conversation with Derville at the dairyman's had changed his character.

At last, having reached the kiosque, he went up to the gazebo, where little rose-windows afforded a view over each lovely landscape of the valley, and where he found his wife seated on a chair. The Countess was gazing at the distance, and preserved a calm countenance, showing that impenetrable face which women can assume when resolved to do their worst. She wiped her eyes as if she had been weeping, and played absently with the pink ribbons of her sash. Nevertheless, in spite of her apparent assurance, she could not help shuddering slightly when she saw before her her venerable benefactor, standing with folded arms, his face pale, his brow stern.

'Madame,' he said, after gazing at her fixedly for a moment and compelling her to blush, 'Madame, I do not curse you — I scorn you. I can now thank the chance that has divided us. I do not feel even a desire for revenge; I no longer love you. I want nothing from you. Live in peace on the strength of my word; it is worth more than the scrawl of all the notaries in Paris. I will never assert my claim to the name I perhaps have made illustrious. I am henceforth but a poor devil named Hyacinthe, who asks no more than his share of the sunshine. — Farewell!'

The Countess threw herself at his feet; she would have detained him by taking his hands, but he pushed her away with disgust, saying:

'Do not touch me!'

The Countess' expression when she heard her husband's retreating steps is quite indescribable. Then, with the deep perspicacity given only by utter villainy, or by fierce worldly selfishness, she knew that she might live in peace on the word and the contempt of this loyal veteran.

Chabert, in fact, disappeared. The dairyman failed in business, and became a hackney-cab driver. The Colonel, perhaps, took up some similar industry for a time. Perhaps, like a stone flung into a chasm, he went falling from ledge to ledge, to be lost in the mire of rags that seethes through the streets of Paris.

Six months after this event, Derville, hearing no more of Colonel Chabert or the Comtesse Ferraud, supposed that they had no doubt come to a compromise, which the Countess, out of revenge, had had arranged by some other lawyer. So one morning he added up the sums he had advanced to the said Chabert with the costs, and begged the Comtesse Ferraud to claim from M. le Comte Chabert the amount of the bill, assuming that she would know where to find her first husband.

The very next day Comte Ferraud's man of business, lately appointed President of the County Court in a town of some importance, wrote this distressing note to Derville:

Monsieur — Madame la Comtesse Ferraud desires me to inform you that your client took complete advantage of your confidence, and that the individual calling himself Comte Chabert has acknowledged that he came forward under false pretences.

Yours, etc., Delbecq

'One comes across people who are, on my honour, too stupid by half,' cried Derville. 'They don't deserve to be Christians! Be humane, generous, philanthropical, and a lawyer, and you are bound to be cheated! There is a piece of business that will cost me two thousand-franc notes!'

Some time after receiving this letter, Derville went to the Palais de Justice in search of a pleader to whom he wished to speak, and who was employed in the Police Court. As chance would have it, Derville went into Court Number 6 at the moment when the Presiding Magistrate was sentencing one Hyacinthe to two months' imprisonment as a vagabond, and subsequently to be taken to the Mendicity House of Detention, a sentence which, by magistrates' law, is equivalent to perpetual imprisonment. On hearing the name of Hyacinthe, Derville looked at the delinquent, sitting between two *gendarmes* on the bench for the accused, and recognized in the condemned man his false Colonel Chabert.

The old soldier was placid, motionless, almost absentminded. In spite of his rags, in spite of the misery stamped on his countenance, it gave evidence of noble pride. His eye had a stoical expression which no magistrate ought to have misunderstood; but as soon as a man has fallen into the hands of justice, he is no more than a moral entity, a matter of law or of fact, just as to statists he has become a zero.

When the veteran was taken back to the lock-up, to be removed later with the batch of vagabonds at that moment at the bar, Derville availed himself of the privilege accorded to lawyers of going wherever they please in the Courts, and followed him to the lock-up, where he stood scrutinizing him for some minutes, as well as the curious crew of beggars among whom he found himself. The passage to the lock-up at that moment afforded one of those spectacles which, unfortunately, neither legislators, nor philanthropists, nor painters, nor writers come to study. Like all the laboratories of the law, this ante-room is a dark and malodorous place; along the walls runs a wooden seat, blackened by the constant presence there of the wretches who come to this meeting-place of every form of social squalor, where not one of them is missing.

A poet might say that the day was ashamed to light up this dreadful sewer through which so much misery flows! There is not a spot on that plank where some crime has not sat, in embryo or matured; not a corner where a man has never stood who, driven to despair by the blight which justice has set upon him after his first fault, has not there begun a career, at the end of which looms the guillotine or the pistol-snap of the suicide. All who fall on the pavement of Paris rebound against these yellow-grey walls, on which a philanthropist who was not a speculator might read a justification of the numerous suicides complained of by hypocritical writers who are incapable of taking a step to prevent them — for that justification is written in that ante-room, like a preface to the dramas of the Morgue, or to those enacted on the Place de la Greve.

At this moment Colonel Chabert was sitting among these men — men with coarse faces, clothed in the horrible livery of misery, and silent at intervals, or talking in a low tone, for three gendarmes on duty paced to and fro, their sabres clattering on the floor.

'Do you recognize me?' said Derville to the old man, standing in front of him.

'Yes, sir,' said Chabert, rising.

'If you are an honest man,' Derville went on in an undertone, 'how could you remain in my debt?'

The old soldier blushed as a young girl might when accused by her mother of a clandestine love affair.

'What! Madame Ferraud has not paid you?' cried he in a loud voice.

'Paid me?' said Derville. 'She wrote to me that you were a swindler.'

The Colonel cast up his eyes in a sublime impulse of horror and imprecation, as if to call heaven to witness to this fresh subterfuge.

'Monsieur,' said he, in a voice that was calm by sheer huskiness, 'get the gendarmes to allow me to go into the lock-up, and I will sign an order which will certainly be honoured.'

At a word from Derville to the sergeant he was allowed to take his client into the room, where Hyacinthe wrote a few lines, and addressed them to the Comtesse Ferraud.

'Send her that,' said the soldier, 'and you will be paid your costs and the money you advanced. Believe me, monsieur, if I have not shown you the gratitude I owe you for your kind offices, it is not the less there,' and he laid his hand on his heart. 'Yes, it is there, deep and sincere. But what can the unfortunate do? They live, and that is all.'

'What!' said Derville. 'Did you not stipulate for an allowance?'

'Do not speak of it!' cried the old man. 'You cannot conceive how deep my contempt is for the outside life to which most men cling. I was suddenly attacked by a sickness — disgust of humanity. When I think that Napoleon is at Saint-Helena, everything on earth is a matter of indifference to me. I can no longer be a soldier; that is my only real grief. After all,' he added with a gesture of childish simplicity, 'it is better to enjoy luxury of feeling than of dress. For my part, I fear nobody's contempt.'

And the Colonel sat down on his bench again.

Derville went away. On returning to his office, he sent Godeschal, at that time his second clerk, to the Comtesse Ferraud, who, on reading the note, at once paid the sum due to Comte Chabert's lawyer.

In 1840, towards the end of June,

Godeschal, now himself an attorney, went to Ris with Derville, to whom he had succeeded. When they reached the avenue leading from the highroad to Bicetre, they saw, under one of the elm-trees by the wayside, one of those old, broken, and hoary paupers who have earned the Marshal's staff among beggars by living on at Bicetre as poor women live on at la Salpetriere. This man, one of the two thousand poor creatures who are lodged in the infirmary for the aged, was seated on a corner-stone, and seemed to have concentrated all his intelligence on an operation well known to these pensioners, which consists in drying their snuffy pocket-handkerchiefs in the sun, perhaps to save washing them. This old man had an attractive countenance. He was dressed in a reddish cloth wrapper-coat which the work-house affords to its inmates, a sort of horrible livery.

'I say, Derville,' said Godeschal to his traveling companion, 'look at that old fellow. Isn't he like those grotesque carved figures we get from Germany? And it is alive, perhaps it is happy.'

Derville looked at the poor man through his eyeglass, and with a little exclamation of surprise he said:

'That old man, my dear fellow, is a whole poem, or, as the romantics say, a drama.

— Did you ever meet the Comtesse Ferraud?'

'Yes; she is a clever woman, and agreeable; but rather too pious,' said Godeschal.

'That old Bicetre pauper is her lawful husband, Comte Chabert, the old Colonel. She has had him sent here, no doubt. And if he is in this workhouse instead of living in a mansion, it is solely because he reminded the pretty Countess that he had taken her, like a hackney cab, on the street. I can remember now the tiger's glare she shot at him at that moment.'

This opening having excited Godeschal's curiosity, Derville related the story here told.

Two days later, on Monday morning, as they returned to Paris, the two friends looked again at Bicetre, and Derville proposed that they should call on Colonel Chabert. Halfway up the avenue they found the old man sitting on the trunk of a felled tree. With his stick in one hand, he was amusing himself with drawing lines in the sand. On looking at him narrowly, they perceived that he had been breakfasting elsewhere than at Bicetre.

'Good-morning, Colonel Chabert,' said Derville.

'Not Chabert! not Chabert! My name is Hyacinthe,' replied the veteran. 'I am no longer a man, I am No. 164, Room 7,' he added, looking at Derville with timid anxiety, the fear of an old man and a child. — 'Are you going to visit the man condemned to death?' he asked after a moment's silence. 'He is not married! He is very lucky!'

'Poor fellow!' said Godeschal. 'Would you like something to buy snuff?'

With all the simplicity of a street Arab, the Colonel eagerly held out his hand to the two strangers, who each gave him a twenty-franc piece; he thanked them with a puzzled look, saying:

'Brave troopers!'

He ported arms, pretended to take aim at them, and shouted with a smile:

'Fire! both arms! *Vive Napoleon!*' And he drew a flourish in the air with his stick.

'The nature of his wound has no doubt made him childish,' said Derville.

'Childish! he?' said another old pauper, who was looking on. 'Why, there are days when you had better not tread on his corns. He is an old rogue, full of philosophy and imagination. But to-day, what can you expect! He has had his Monday treat. — He was here, monsieur, so long ago as 1820. At that time a Prussian officer, whose chaise was crawling up the hill of Villejuif, came by on foot. We two were together, Hyacinthe and I, by the roadside. The officer, as he walked, was talking to another, a Russian, or some animal of the same species, and when the Prussian saw the old boy, just to make fun, he said to him, 'Here is an old cavalry man who must have been at Rossbach.' — 'I was too young to be there,' said Hyacinthe. 'But I was at Jena.' And the Prussian made off pretty quick, without asking any more questions.'

'What a destiny!' exclaimed Derville. 'Taken out of the Foundling Hospital to die in the Infirmary for the Aged, after helping Napoleon between whiles to conquer Egypt and Europe. — Do you know, my dear fellow,' Derville went on after a pause, 'there are in modern society three men who can never think well of the world — the priest, the doctor, and the man of law? And they wear black robes, perhaps because they are in mourning for every virtue and every illusion. The most hapless of the three is the lawyer. When a man comes in search of the priest, he is prompted by repentance, by remorse, by beliefs which make him interesting, which elevate him and comfort the soul of the intercessor whose task will bring him a sort of gladness; he purifies, repairs and reconciles. But we lawyers, we see the same evil feelings repeated again and again, nothing can correct them; our offices are sewers which can never be cleansed.

'How many things have I learned in the

exercise of my profession! I have seen a father die in a garret, deserted by two daughters, to whom he had given forty thousand francs a year! I have known wills burned; I have seen mothers robbing their children, wives killing their husbands, and working on the love they could inspire to make the men idiotic or mad, that they might live in peace with a lover. I have seen women teaching the child of their marriage such tastes as must bring it to the grave in order to benefit the child of an illicit affection. I could not tell you all I have seen, for I have seen crimes against which justice is impotent. In short, all the horrors that romancers suppose they have invented are still below the truth. You will know something of these pretty things; as for me, I am going to live in the country with my wife. I have a horror of Paris.'

'I have seen plenty of them already in Desroches' office,' replied Godeschal.